D0860125

STRAND PRICE

Also by Carolyn Cooke

The Bostons

Daughters of the Revolution

Daughters

of the

Revolution

{ A Novel }

CAROLYN COOKE

ALFRED A. KNOPF

New York

2011

THIS IS A BORZOI BOOK
PUBLISHED BY ALFRED A. KNOPF

www.aaknopf.com

Library of Congress Cataloging-in-Publication Data
Cooke, Carolyn, [date]
Daughters of the Revolution / Carolyn Cooke. — 1st ed.
p. cm.
ISBN 978-0-307-59473-0
1. School principals—Fiction. 2. Preparatory school students—Fiction. 3. Preparatory schools—New England—Fiction. 4. New England—Fiction. 5. School integration—Fiction. 6. Social conflict—Fiction. 7. Teenage boys—Fiction. 8. Teenage girls—Fiction. I. Title.
PS3553.O55495D38 2011
813'.6—dc22 2011002743

Jacket image: *Falling in Trees 6, 2007*
© Elijah Gowin. Courtesy Robert Mann Gallery, New York
Jacket design by Chip Kidd

Manufactured in the United States of America
First Edition

For Randall Babtkis
and for Zack and Callie Babtkis

Contents

The Saved Man *1*

The Big Bang *23*

The Strangler *37*

The Seducer *43*

God-Father *51*

The First Girl *57*

The Greedy Girl *71*

Why We Love Hell *81*

A Cold Case *85*

EV in New York *101*

The Graduate *119*

The Ordination of Women *123*

Himself *139*

The Death of God *147*

Souls of the Drowned *165*

1963

The Saved Man

Heck Hellman, walking home from gross anatomy and his basement cadaver, felt buoyed by the sleazy promise of spring: a yellow sky above, the gray snow on the ground turned to a slush that poured sloppily down the storm drains to the ocean.

He climbed the stairs up the side of the house, calling their new kitten's name—*Graham Greene!*—into the empty air. Mrs. O'Greefe, the landlady, immediately appeared behind him, her dress pulling tight against her body, and told him cats ran away all the time, hid out. "They're like children," she said. "They'll suffer and die rather than show they want you."

"Do they?" Heck asked.

"That they do, Mr. Hellman."

Mrs. O'Greefe's husband was in prison—"incarcerated," Mrs. O'Greefe said—for killing a man in a bar under "compromised" circumstances. Mrs. O'Greefe had once owned her own hair salon in town, but she was now reduced to renting out half her house, living downstairs in one bedroom with a hot plate and a shower stall, watching Heck's small family revel in the comforts she'd once known. She longed to have her husband back, she told Heck one night when, drunk, she came up the back stairs to change a fuse. Sometimes she couldn't sleep, thinking about it. Who wouldn't miss marriage? she asked Heck gently, her eyes red. She wished she still had it all.

A dish of milk sat on the porch, looking rained on and sooty. Heck's daughter, EV, insisted on feeding the kitten great troughs of milk, and used the stuff up that way. The sinister look of the milk in the bowl made Heck imagine Graham Greene had run afoul of a car, as their previous cats had done.

It was a shabby house, all they could afford. The staircase up the side separated Heck and his wife Lil's quarters from Mrs. O'Greefe's. Just beyond the storm door, Lil stirred Rob Roys in an old mayonnaise jar. EV, three years old, knelt on the floor and stared deeply into the rubber plant. Heck caught the ghost of his own face in the glass.

Part of him belonged here—to this family, in this kitchen. The checkerboard flooring ran partway up the walls. *"Coved linoleum,"* Mrs. O'Greefe had told them with pride before they took the rental. "Never any water damage!"

He closed the door behind him and set down his briefcase—his father's briefcase, too good to throw away, though his father had repaired the broken handle with a wire hanger and the case was no longer handsome, or easy to hold. A tang of formaldehyde and phenol hung in the air, which came, Heck realized, from himself.

The child looked up and ran toward him, leaping through the air. Lil called, "Careful, Eavieeee!" as she always did, drawing out the name, and as always he dropped the wire-handled briefcase and caught his daughter in his arms. Her hands attached to his face like suction cups. Then Lil handed Heck his glass and kissed him; the first sip of scotch melted on his tongue.

In the kitchen, Lil stuffed green peppers with hash. EV dropped to the floor and played with two tiny dolls in the potted rubber plant. She moved them around in the dirt and spoke in each of their voices.

"I'm a nickel," one doll said.

"I'm a penny," said the other.

"No sign of the kitten?" Heck asked Lil. She shook her head, but EV looked up from her dolls and said, "I see him."

"Graham Greene isn't here," Lil told her gently. "Remember we looked for him outside?"

"I see him," EV insisted.

"Where is he, then?" asked Heck, smiling.

"Gone," EV said.

"But where has he gone?"

"Graham Greene gone *dead*!"

"He isn't dead, honey," Lil said. "He's just out and about."

Lil shot Heck a tragic look and sipped her drink. She was wearing dungarees and an old navy wool sweater. He'd knit the sweater himself when he was fifteen; his mother had taught him how. Both the dungarees and the sweater looked as if they could slip off her body without her unfastening anything. Two chopsticks held her dark hair up, but barely.

"So," she said, sipping. "Hard day at the corpse?"

Heck didn't like the way she referred to Mrs. X., his cadaver, as a corpse. Mrs. X.'s face was always covered with a cloth, but he'd removed her lungs and ovaries, studied the structure of her ruined knee, and squinted through sections of her circulatory system like a boy looking down the dark tube of a seashell.

"So," he said, "tomorrow I'm meeting Rebozos to see that German kayak."

"Really, Heck? In this weather?"

"We might take it out for a few minutes along the shore."

"I wish you wouldn't."

"Rebozos wants us to have it while he's in Mexico this summer. We could have good times with a boat."

"With a *baby*," Lil added witheringly.

"EV's not a baby. Are you a baby, EV?"

"I'm your baby," EV said, her voice going up like a rocket. Then her voice came back down and she said, "And I am Mommy's baby."

"I asked you not to call me Mommy," Lil said. "I don't like it."

"What do you want her to call you?" Heck asked, surprised.

Lil touched the chopsticks in her hair. "You can call me Mei-Mei."

"My-My-My," said EV.

"See?" said Lil.

Heck got down on the floor and played with EV. He lay on his back and lifted her so that her round stomach rested against the bottoms of his feet. He spread her little arms across his hands. "Airplane!" she shouted. A line of drool dropped from her mouth onto Heck's cheek.

"Mrs. O'Greefe told me today that a certain person might be p-a-r-o-l-e-d and coming home—coming here," Lil said. "I think she's not as happy about it as she lets on." They'd joked before about the murderer returning: "Over my dead body," Lil had said.

"That could be arranged," he'd said.

Mrs. O'Greefe had made her husband's felony sound like a failure of communication, one she expected Lil and Heck to understand, like a political crime, or a tragic misunderstanding between black and Irish. She made it sound as if Mr. O'Greefe was not only the perpetrator of the crime he had committed but also the victim.

When Heck brought the new kitten home, Lil had been on a Graham Greene jag. She'd read *The Man Within*, *The Third Man*, *The End of the Affair*, *The Quiet American* and *The Heart of the Matter*, all in the time it had taken Heck to get halfway through *The Power and the Glory*. When she'd finished, she'd looked around hungrily, and he'd given his book over.

Heck went out one last time and called unsuccessfully for

the kitten in the dark. What kitten ever came when called? Then he brushed his teeth, stripped down to his shorts, climbed into bed and waited for Lil to finish her drink. They took turns in the evenings, reading to EV and putting her to bed. His wife called the quarter hour that followed this ritual—the dregs of her second Rob Roy—the "moment of bliss" she needed to survive, but it seemed less like bliss to Heck than a romantic sorrow he tried to avoid. He heard the scratchy record playing Billie Holiday, and the ice knocking in her glass as she lifted it, then set it down. (The blond-wood table wore her rings.) He skimmed the *Globe* in bed while he waited for her, but his mind was on the contemptuous spit of rain against the windows. Massachusetts had consecrated its first black bishop, who was also to be the summer minister on Capawak Island. The Boston Strangler had struck again, an older woman, sixty-three. Total annihilation was mutually assured: Anyone could push a button and destroy everyone else. A draft of air carried the scent of Lil's perfume. Heck tried to imagine everything he knew and cared for blown to bits—baseball, his wife's mouth, his wife, his baby daughter—atomized. He looked across the bed to the blocky tower of her reading: *Tropic of Cancer*—a dirty book, she promised—*Ship of Fools,* the Graham Greene novels. Whenever he finally finished a book Lil said had changed her life, she was on to something else.

He lay on his back, stroking himself and thinking about the morning. The plan was to meet Archer Rebozos at the boathouse at seven. Then, if it wasn't raining, they'd take the kayak along the shore off Wilde Point. This is what he'd told Lil. In fact, Rebozos had talked about going farther, eight miles out, to Capawak—a classic test for Wampanoag braves. Heck hadn't mentioned the eight-mile trip. He knew Lil wouldn't like it.

Heck had offered to take sandwiches. Otherwise, Rebozos might suggest going out for lunch, and Heck had just a dollar in his wallet until Friday. It was a hell of a way to live, Lil supporting all three of them with her job as a detective for the Better Business Bureau. He was only near the end of his first year of medical school, an old man at twenty-nine. He'd wanted to be a minister, had flirted with divinity until his mid-twenties. He still believed, somehow, in it. ("That's a strange idea," his mother said when he confessed.) For Heck not to be too much like his father, that's what his mother wanted.

Now Heck carried his father's briefcase. He carried his father's thermos, so he wouldn't have to spend a nickel at the coffee shop. Heck's father had been an extravagant figure who always bought the best of everything and wore it to shreds. When he died, at forty-nine, Heck's mother could not bring herself to give away his shoes and bespoke suits. The wingtips Heck wore every day to school were thinned by wear but beautifully soft. Old as they were—Heck's father had died the spring Heck graduated from high school, twelve years ago, and the shoes had been ancient then—they still smelled faintly of the citrusy chemical his father had used to clean them, the secret of which had gone down with him.

Now Heck was not anything like his father. He studied physiology and gross anatomy and worked on Mrs. X., peeling away her epidermis, dermis and subcutaneous tissue to examine the loaded liver, the black lungs. The work was different from what he'd expected; it shocked him. He had not yet seen her face.

He wanted a day on the water—the challenge, the experience of the crossing. Lil liked, on Saturdays, to go swimming at the Y pool while he made French toast with EV. Lil no longer spoke about becoming a professional swimmer, which had been anyway a dream. He couldn't blame her for wanting things. He wanted things, too: He wanted her. They had always rubbed up against each other well. She'd dated his roommate first, then someone else he knew. At first, she had pretended not to like him. Walking by him at a dance, she'd bumped into his chair, which had produced an encouraging buzz between them. One evening, he'd called her up—"Is this Lily Field?"—and invited her out for a drink. To his surprise, she didn't pretend to be busy; she didn't make him wait. They went to a cheap place on Charles Street. He never had money except the disheveled-looking bills his mother flung at him at lunch on Sunday afternoons. He threw these untidy dollars on the bar, glad to see them go.

"You've brought me to a tawdry barroom," Lil accused him. She was beautiful, her hair held up somehow by two chopsticks; she laughed at him. She took his hand and then—not that night, but the next one—she kissed him at the door of the apartment building where she lived with three other girls in a demimonde of ashtrays and underpants. She kissed him under the stone lintel, hard on the lips. She demanded that he talk. She gave him books to read, and she swam for two hours every day. He began to think about what he could tell his mother—because from his mother's point of view, Lil was not better than Maeve, the last girl he'd brought home.

In the end, they eloped—she took a long weekend from school and they borrowed Rebozos's car and drove to Elkton, Maryland, where they were married by a justice of the peace with a scar across his neck. Lil wore a silk suit—a cheap silk suit, she said disdainfully—and afterward they spent the night in a crumbly hotel Lil found charming. They slept together, ate pancakes, drank stingers in the lounge, then drove home at the last possible moment, leaving at four in the morning so Lil could be back by ten for her class, The Radical Dramas of Bertolt Brecht.

Lil had savings, "money from my Grammy," she said. She used it for a deposit and several months' rent on a two-room apartment on the wrong side of the Hill. Here Lil produced the empty mayonnaise jar in which he stirred their first Rob Roys, and she began to cook—BLTs and Welsh rarebit. It was better than life. They each played new parts, performing scenes of domestic comfort and sexual freedom. They met at three for what Lil called "love in the afternoon." Then she stood in her baby-doll pajamas over the stove while he mixed drinks. At home, his mother nagged him about medical school, why he must become a doctor—he must do it for himself. How proud his father and grandfather would be! In the apartment, Lil drew him out and encouraged him, until he felt medical school had been his own idea and there was no danger of his life veering in a direction he did not want to go.

Their daughter had not yet learned to breathe fluently. Her breathing lacked some essential quality—continuity, rhythm—every breath was different. He wondered at this lack of organization, focus, will or instinct. Heck could hear Lil now, in EV's room, her respiration loud and instructional.

Lil walked into the bedroom, said, "Hello, finally," then undressed. She peeled off the turtleneck sweater and pulled her blue jeans down over her hips without unzipping them. She slid the chopsticks from her hair, which fell darkly around her shoulders, climbed into bed, laid her head on his arm. He pressed against her. "You want to do something?" he asked, parting the curtain of hair with his fingers and whispering into her ear. He reached his other hand between her legs, guided by heat.

She answered by climbing up, sliding on like a ring. He closed his eyes, then opened them. Light from the ceiling fixture poured down on her shoulders, her muscles long and elastic from swimming. Her face looked elegant and remote as she began to move. Her teeth gleamed.

A fearful glow of fertility surrounded her. If Heck asked whether she'd put in the Thing—the rubber cap that pushed unpleasantly back at him—she might stop to check again on EV, who might wake up. Or he could take her as she was and run the risk.

He received the pressure of her body against his, pressed back. She opened more to receive him, and he felt he could expand infinitely to fill the space she'd made. He played with this sensation, tested its boundaries. She cried out—but softly—and he rolled on top of her. Her eyes closed and she disappeared into a private zone, which freed them. Then she came, holding him tightly, with her legs wrapped around his back, her face flushed and blurry. The walls of her body beat against him in delicate paroxysms. He thrust up into her several times before pulling away, and she returned to the present, to the bedroom, to her usual intense focus. She slithered down under the sheet, where she kissed and licked him until pins rose up from underneath his skin and he exploded.

A gray, ordinary darkness woke him. His wife lay beside him in a fetal ball. He dressed in his warmest, lightest clothes—twill pants, thermal shirt, varsity jacket, crew socks and sneakers—and walked into the kitchen. The sky turned pink at the edges and the thermometer on the porch read thirty-nine degrees. The kitten's milk had turned opalescent in the rain, which continued to fall lightly into the bare maples.

He plugged in the percolator, which he'd loaded with coffee the night before, and heated water in the kettle to prime the thermos. He mixed two tins of deviled ham with mayonnaise and pickle relish and made sandwiches, which he wrapped neatly in waxed paper; he didn't want Rebozos to feel he was slumming. Heck wished he had homemade cookies to put into the lunch, something beyond price. But Lil didn't make cookies; she didn't keep sweets in the house. Two apples sat in a bowl on the kitchen table. They'd begun to shrivel, but they might revive in the cold. The milk carton in the refrigerator was nearly empty, so he cooked and ate his oats with water. Rebozos liked milk in his coffee, so Heck heated the rest of it in a Revere pan, poured the milk and coffee into the thermos and tightened the suction.

He brushed his teeth, then stopped in his daughter's room. EV's adenoidal breathing sounded disorganized; her eyelashes flickered in a dream. Heck leaned down and kissed her cheek.

He whispered good-bye to Lil and kissed her on the mouth. Her hands reached for his face. "Have fun. Come home," she said, eyes still closed. He took the Rambler, which would pin her close to home for the day. Usually, Heck appreciated the simplicity of their arrangements, and would rather do without than spend. But this morning, money seemed all that held him back from being fully himself, his fear that Archer Rebozos would say, "To hell with sandwiches, Heck; let's have a hot lunch at Drake's," the fear he couldn't pay his way. Not a fear, a fact. He owed the future. Even before his father died, Heck had been a scholarship boy. His mother worked in the Goode School office. She ate milk toast and dressed in castoffs from her well-heeled friends in town, whose tickets to Symphony Hall she snared when they got cancer or ran away. But she sent him to college, "the best there is," she said proudly. Sundays when he went over for lunch, she threw dollar bills at him or stuffed them in his pockets. When Lil complained about money, Heck felt guilty about his mother, who lived on less.

The fan blew tepid air and the faulty timing belt eased into a rhythm. He hoped they would take the kayak out. Heck liked games, rules, training, a definite opponent, a goal. He turned the wipers off, willing the day to clear. He drove for a few minutes, his vision slurry, then turned them on again.

In his eagerness, he'd come too early. Now he walked up and down in front of the locked-up boathouse, trying to keep warm. After twenty minutes, he went back to his car and poured out a cup of milky coffee. He held the hot cup in his hands briefly, then rolled down the window and poured the coffee on the ground.

A taxi pulled up beside the boathouse and a young man wearing a waterproof windbreaker and holding a duffel bag climbed out. Heck jumped out of the car with his pack and ran toward him.

"Hey, Hellman," Rebozos said.

"You didn't have to get a car," Heck said. "I would have come for you."

Rebozos grinned. "I didn't come from home," he said.

A few white clouds opened up, revealing orange light behind. "Weather's clearing," Heck said casually.

Rebozos looked at the sky, then slapped the trunk of the taxi as if it were the rump of a horse; obediently, it drove away. He set the duffel bag on the ground, unzipped it and brought out a ring of keys. Then he walked away from Heck down a gangway into the boathouse. A moment later the wide door groaned and cracked open. Heck tossed his pack over his shoulder—it wasn't heavy—and jogged down the gangway.

The kayak sat on a rack—sleek, engineered, German. The green trim looked wet. Rebozos's father had arranged to have it brought into the country. Heck ran a hand along the hull and a current passed through him. He wanted what this boat wanted.

"We could take her out on the water," Rebozos said.

"We could do that," Heck agreed.

"You're not dressed for the weather, Hellman."

"You're not, either."

"I don't care. I don't have a wife and a kid."

"She'll take care of me if I catch pneumonia."

The boathouse yielded one life jacket, and Rebozos cursed the boathouse. "Stupid, stupid—" he said. "They're all on the other side." For a moment it seemed they could not go; then, out of a kind of honor both men understood too well to protest against, they said nothing. Rebozos tossed the life jacket into the hold with Heck's thermos and the sandwiches. Rebozos had everything ready, a sea chart and a guidebook open to a page that read, "Wilde Point to Maude's Duff by Paddling: Classic Route of Wampanoag Braves."

Heck felt lucky to be part of it.

Eight miles across. They'd warm up while they paddled, then load the kayak onto the ferry and ride back. He'd tell Lil about it after they had a drink, or after dinner. It depended—on her. Maybe he would never tell.

"You first," Rebozos said. Heck climbed forward, splashing his sneakers. Rebozos ran through the water up to his shins, pushed off and jumped aboard.

The ferry beat them out. Her iron jaw opened for passengers, crates of oranges, bags of mail and the short line of cars that breathed clouds of exhaust. Then she detached herself from the dock and headed from Penzance Point to Capawak, the island where, three hundred years before, the Native Americans had helped the English survive the winter. Heck and Rebozos had no choice but to follow in her matronly wake.

They paddled southeast. Heck drove the kayak forward.

"I went fishing here once with the Head," Rebozos shouted. "We caught sea bass and pogy."

The sun shot through a bank of silver clouds. "I spent last night with a French teacher from Wilde High," Rebozos confided. "Ooh la la!" He made another remark, which Heck didn't hear. The ferry slid through the water and cut them loose. The shore dissolved. The paddle's blade sliced through the water like a hot knife through cake.

At school—at Goode—Heck and Rebozos had been part of a brilliant class of boys, the kind of boys the Head mentioned when he spoke against the possibility of coeducation—why it would never happen. From the outside, Heck and Rebozos and virtually all the boys shared an almost familial resemblance: Their teeth were organized into martial ranks by orthodontia, and they wore their button-down shirts buttoned up. (Heck and Rebozos veered from the norm in that both were left-handed, so the master usually segregated them at the short end of a work-table to prevent their elbows from knocking against the elbows of the right-handed boys as they wrote in their blue books.)

Some of the boys dated girls in the summer, held hands in the movies or skinny-dipped in a quarry, but school demanded the better part of their lives, and it was here, in tutorial rooms, in the gymnasium and the fields beyond, that they recognized themselves in the traditions of the school. They'd been chosen to run the world, but first they had to read *King Lear* and *Heart of Darkness,* pass trigonometry, write an argumentative essay in six paragraphs, translate a hundred lines of Virgil and dissect a fetal pig.

Heck was a day boy; Rebozos boarded. The first year, Rebozos never went home—not one time. It was even unclear where "home" might be, since the house on the island had to be closed up for winter. Rebozos's parents hid away in Arizona or the West Indies, or his mother needed to recuperate from some not-too-serious affliction, an infection in her eye or a touch of eczema or hysteria, that made it impractical for Rebozos to join them.

The Head—Goddard Byrd—asked Heck's mother to do something for the school and invite Rebozos to spend Thanksgiving break with the Hellmans. She said yes, of course, although the prospect of a visitor made her anxious. Heck's father was still alive, but she managed it, as if she entertained a constant stream of boys. She sat at the cherry table with her half-glasses on the end of her nose. "The Rebozos boy is used to the best of everything," she said. She bought butter and real maple syrup from Vermont, put strawberry jam in a clay pot. She bought wine and fresh-ground coffee and tomatoes.

For privacy, Heck's mother and father had separate bedrooms, but for the duration of Rebozos's visit they arranged to sleep together, which produced a strange vibration in the air. Heck's mother greeted the boys with cookies and hot chocolate and fussed over them, until Heck suggested that he and Rebozos take a walk. They trekked down Otis Street, past faded Salem-style houses and maple trees with hand-shaped leaves in reds and ochers, and Rebozos talked. He talked like no boy Heck had ever heard. Most boys talked about the sports they played, their heroics on fields and courts, about girls and the uselessness of Latin, about whether a supreme being (God, Vishnu, Krishna, Yahweh, Allah) existed in a literal form. Most boys were also at ease without talking. None of this applied to Rebozos, who talked as if he had never lived among ordinary people.

Rebozos did not go often to Capawak Island; he'd spent last summer in Europe and what he called "the Near East." His father sent letters to banks, and Rebozos took himself on a tour of London, Paris, the Dordogne, Florence, Rome, Athens, the Aegean Islands and Istanbul. But a Greek island, that's where he'd live if he could. "What would you do there?" Heck asked him, curious not just about Rebozos and Greece but about what it might be possible to do.

"I would do everything," Rebozos said, "*hic et ubique.*"

In Paris, Rebozos had sex with a prostitute. His father arranged it, booked him into a certain hotel, where Rebozos waited for a knock on the door. Her name was Jeanne—*Zhann*—or so she said. Rebozos drank a brandy at the café downstairs beforehand, which produced a vision: He was an actor in a play and his part was simply to play a role, adding whatever of himself he could—nothing Shakespeare didn't say better. He became human when he fucked her; he entered the consciousness of man.

In Greece, Rebozos said, he met Greek boys who had done it with older men.

"How do you know? How did you talk to them?" Heck asked.

"In broken classical Greek."

They walked all the way to town. Rebozos led them into St. Vitus to look at the stained glass, although he noticed immediately that the landscape windows didn't really show the iridescent quality of Tiffany's "favrile" glass. One portrait, beautifully colored, showed a woman weeping; the face and hands and aspects of the robe were overpainted to capture expressive detail. Rebozos showed Heck how to look for the floating of lead and solder; then they walked around the common, which held, Rebozos said, the dusky yellow that Childe Hassam caught in his famous painting—"a modest petticoat of yellow gunpowder." Then he talked about architecture and Unitarians, until suddenly it was dark. Heck became so caught up in it all, he didn't realize how long they'd been gone. He worried out loud about the time and his mother. She would have been frantic since the minute they walked out the door.

Rebozos simply leaned into the street and hailed a cab. Everything he did was easy.

It was easy to be drawn to money, as if it were a quality of character. Heck felt drawn to Rebozos's generous, untroubled spirit, for example. "Come out to the island for the weekend," Rebozos once said—they were in college—and they took the ferry together. As if Rebozos could really know these people, his parents—how could he? Yet the chintz-covered couch held him in a familiar way; the dogs on the lawn knew him and liked him.

The Rebozos family lived in silence and space. Mrs. Rebozos wrote articles analyzing the condition of women in various cultures in the American Southwest and the West Indies; Dr. Rebozos worked upstairs, behind a closed door, on matters of state. They gathered for lunch and dinner like an electron cloud around a nucleus, then dissipated. In the evenings, two living rooms contained two fires, and sometimes no one was there at all. In the mornings, Mrs. Snow put out coffee and whitefish for anyone who wanted it and then withdrew, leaving an elegant vacancy. Heck and Rebozos went outside one foggy morning and picked mushrooms—blewits, Rebozos said, *Clitocybe nuda*!—unusual in this season. (Heck knew nothing about mushrooms, but he trusted Rebozos.)

Heck had brought them all wool scarves he had knit himself: royal blue for Mrs. Rebozos, deep gray for Mr. Rebozos, and crimson for his friend. "You made this?" Rebozos asked, holding the scarf reverently across his hands. During the long weekend Heck spent with them, Mrs. Rebozos wore her scarf constantly—wrapped around her sweater's neck, around the collar of her bathrobe.

They played tennis on the Rebozoses' clay court and Heck won every set. "Cut me some slack, for Christ's sake," Rebozos said. And Heck laughed, disbelieving. No one had ever asked him to be less than he was.

Another day, they walked along the edge of some rocky cliffs as the sun set. Rebozos wore a cashmere sweater and sunglasses. He pointed out mushrooms in the grass: "Milk caps, witches' hats."

Heck and Rebozos squatted at the edge of a pool that ran off into the ocean. Squatted, because of damp grass, and then, as they talked, sat, their khaki pants gathering moisture. Rebozos gazed through his dark glasses at the ocean and confessed a secret: "I have a young daughter I haven't met. She was born six months ago, in the islands. She worked for my parents at their place there. You'll disapprove, Heck. The mother—my lover—is a Negro woman. I suppose I loved her. She never told me about the pregnancy until after the baby was born. Stupid, stupid. But what can you do?"

Wind—had the ferry blocked it?—blew through Heck's varsity jacket and used the resistance of his body to press the boat back toward shore, though there was no shore, no distance, just a bed of gray scallops over which he and Rebozos jangled. The sky glowed metallically and a fiery light poured across the surface of the water. Heck's paddles struck the surface like matchsticks. He blinked away ice. He was a machine, made to go forward, to stroke and stroke. The plan became less important—lunch on the ferry, arriving, returning, having a drink with Lil later, telling or not telling her what he had done. The subject of the day had changed to something unsayable. Heck's arms felt stronger than when they'd first started out—his muscles hot, greased. The ocean toyed with them, batted them off course and then pretended to leave them alone, lifting and dropping the boat as casually as a gull dropping a mussel on a granite shelf. Heck wiped some moisture from his face and saw red; his tongue must be bleeding. In a pause between the undemocratic waves, he turned and saw that Rebozos had removed the life jacket from the hold and put it on.

A mass of shore lay ahead, and sometimes it did not lie ahead. Rain fell from the gray sky and drizzled down Heck's head and face. His eyes stung, ached and fooled him. Here stood Mad Rock, an almost vertical pile. A cormorant with a gaping wound in its head looked down sadly on the men in the boat. "We have to stop," Heck shouted. "I've got to fix this old bird."

"I want to eat," Rebozos called up from behind.

"I brought sandwiches and coffee."

"After this hell? I want a hot lunch and a drink."

Heck had the stronger arm. He put in at the rock, stepped out of the kayak and lifted the cormorant—its body stiff and its eyes dull—in his arms. He held his hand tightly over the wound until the bird relaxed and draped its long black neck against Heck's shoulder. Soon it revived; its body began to hum like a machine and it slipped its wing under his arm. Wings were arms, Heck saw, and arms wings. The long bones and the blue-black feathers fit perfectly. That was it, exactly. The way out of this was up.

Rebozos, still wearing the orange life vest, knit a bandage with silver needles and thin white yarn. "I've shot a cat for supper," he called out.

The cormorant flew straight up and away from them. Heck paddled on, making up the time he'd lost. His head felt light. He would not mention the life vest; it was beneath him. (But he and Rebozos might not be friends after this.) He rose above it and flew along the shoreline. He saw open land where a fire pond looked like a blue bladder in a brown body. He saw fins in the water, slicing through the offshore swells. He saw Mad Rock, two miles out, and two figures in a kayak, paddling away from the rock; one of them wore an orange life jacket. He saw a baseball sailing into the air. He saw his mother covering her mouth with her hand—was she ashamed?—and Lil's face, smiling at him, one of her front teeth folded slightly over the other. He saw Mrs. O'Greefe, holding her arms against her chest, her dress transparent in the rain. Water ran backward up his face, forcing tears into his eyes. Mrs. X. sat up and removed the cloth from her face. The pilot dipped, rode first on one wing, then on the other. For an instant, Heck saw an impossible thing: a kitten with large ears and almond-shaped eyes standing on the rock. "Where did you learn to fly?" the passenger asked the pilot.

"I am a Wampanoag brave," the pilot said. "This is our ancestral air."

The wing dipped, and when it rose again, the kitten had disappeared.

She wrapped herself in her thrift-store kimono and walked to the kitchen to pour a cup of coffee. But the milk carton stood empty on the counter and the percolator sucked in the brew with an esophageal hiss. She left Heck's little mess for later and looked in on EV, who also breathed as if she were drinking through a straw.

Back in bed, she planned her escape, an hour of reading. But Heck's shy eyes watched her in the dark and made her wet with desire. She saw herself through his eyes, from the outside; the way he looked at her, the way men looked at her, helped her to see herself this way. O'Greefe, cheap as a two-cent stamp, had the heat cranked down, but the bed held a memory of warmth. The kimono, silky but not silk, also held her own heat in. She ran her hands over her skin, her breasts larger than before EV, and saw herself as if she were a bird flying overhead and looking down at a woman unfolding under her unfolding kimono. Even her mouth felt aroused.

"Veux-tu que je débarrasse la table?" she whispered, the language all silk and velvet and pearls.

The apartment roared like a hollow shell. She folded and unfolded herself, lying tangled under the warm, ugly Hudson Bay blanket her Uncle Frank had given them for a wedding present, a practical and insinuating gift, made to last.

The spongy mattress (Heck's parents' ancient nuptial bed) held her in a watery embrace. She wanted a lot. She wanted more. She had everything she needed. She turned her head, opened her mouth and swallowed—like a pill—her little cry of ecstasy.

Wind whipped the water up in peaks. The Brewsters' sitter shook sand from the blanket and packed the canvas boat bag, preparing to take her two charges home. She'd brought them to the beach with a thermos of hot chocolate and they'd made a castle, although the sand pecked at their eyes and faces, and their hands went numb from digging moats and pressing cold sand into turrets. Just now, she'd caught the older one, the boy, watching her when she squatted among the rocks to pee. She'd made them put their hands over their eyes and sing "Frère Jacques" in a round so they wouldn't hear her splashing, but this one, his eyes were wide open.

The boy was also the first to see the two men spill into the gray water about two hundred yards offshore. He pointed, and the sitter doubted what she saw—two men? No direct signal, no sound told her that what she saw was true. But the boy, who had the empathy of a frog, pointed gravely, and the girl cried out, "Two mens in the water!"

The sitter pulled off her red sweatshirt and the two shirts she wore under it and stood before the children for a terrifying instant in her bra.

They stood in front of her with their mouths open. "Go—tell—run!" she said, and ran, right up against the waves and through the whitecaps. Then she dove and swam.

She was not just any sitter, but a certified lifeguard, covered with a rubbery layer of fat. Cold and water did not scare her. Even when she could no longer feel her body, even low in the water, when she could not see where she was going, she swam in a line, the water like fire at her feet.

One man touched the sides of the boat. She saw long, feminine fingers spread on the bow, not really holding on, just touching it. She could not see his head or face. Then his fingers lost contact with the boat and sank into the water. The other man, buoyed up by a life jacket, flailed toward her.

Heck saw the shore. He saw a woman on the beach, who wore red clothing and held, in each of her hands, the hand of a child. He paddled more shrewdly, to trick the ocean. He would not affront it directly; he would come in from one side. The gray shore lay just ahead and the woman standing on the shore appeared bright, like a red flag. She was the sight Heck set his eye on. His breath crackled in his chest like leaves on fire. Between strokes, he felt Rebozos's wild stirring of the water. They might not be friends after this.

1968

THE BIG BANG

He begins with a bang at the center of his story. It's spring of that revolutionary year, not too far in. Meringues of snow line the sidewalks, but a freshness cuts the air. Goddard Byrd—known to his friends and enemies as "God"—has just emerged from an afternoon at the Parker House Hotel, a virile, uncircumcised male of his class, upbringing and era. His prostate gland and his *praeputium* have not yet been removed, and he is unburdened, just now, of Puritanism's load. He has drunk a glass of gin, then lain with Mrs. Viktor Rebozos—whom he must remember to call Aileen—and both of them are better for this exercise.

In bed, she tells him he is a bear, all paws and claws. She insults him, purrs, climbs on top. She wants to know if he could be any wild animal, which would he be?

An animal? He would be a tiger!

(She would be a gazelle.)

He likes himself better this way, his natural shyness tempered by adrenaline. She is more flexible than he, more at ease, depending on the occasion—more pliable. Women *are* pliable, he thinks; they revel in the shifting relations required by husbands, children, lovers, others. (How can this be a matter of opinion?) He can't tell Mrs. Rebozos these things; she might eat him alive.

They lie together in the fading afternoon light, the March grisaille. "The most beautiful words in the English language are *sex in the afternoon*," she tells him, and he can't, in the moment, find reason to correct her. Mrs. Rebozos's tongue darts suddenly across his left nipple, and God rises with an animal roar, his body fire and ice.

She smiles. "I read that in *The Kama Sutra of Vatsyayana*."

"Do it again," says God.

Her tongue and lips move excruciatingly over his body, describing ancient erotic techniques from the Orient. He rises obediently as a snake in a basket. God lifts his head to look at her, and feels an organ breach (liver? spleen?). She is so gamine, indeed! She looks like a boy. Almost. Short hair. Hoops in her ears. All of it signifying what? Maybe nothing.

Eventually, he pins her to her back, which she seems to enjoy, and humps her in the familiar way, running breathlessly toward a goal, which he reaches.

"You're beginning to get it, my earnest missionary," she tells him afterward. "Let's hope it's not too late."

They share a plate of cold roast beef, a famous roll. Naked, quivering a little, she wraps a blue knit scarf around her shoulders. "My dark secret," she says. "All my life I've been drawn to misogynist coots like you. Like a taste for black coffee—incredible when you think about it." Even God is surprised that a free-spirited woman such as Mrs. Rebozos would so defiantly stand beside an old man, in his shadow, eat meat with him and be his prize!

"I have to go," he says into her ear. "You could stay all afternoon; you could have a bath."

"Just a quick shower," she says. "I have a women's thing. Last week, we inspected our cervixes. Mine looked like an eye. It *blinked*."

God tries to conceal his horror. At three, he descends, leaving Mrs. Rebozos to enjoy the rented room, whose extravagant price stabs him when he thinks of it. (In spite of the evidence, he imagines her as feminine, passive, mysterious and inert. Women in their beds, Rorschach blots on luminous sheets.)

He advances through the lobby and rolls into the street like a well-oiled man on wheels. The atmosphere of hostility and depravity beyond the doors of the Parker House stings him like a slap. The street is filthy; even the city fathers are off their game, lax or stoned. Girls in paper dresses—temporary dresses for temporary girls—giggle at him. He's harmless, they think, the last of a dying breed.

God passes gently into a haze of mustard-purple-maroon and marijuana fumes. In spite of the expense of the hotel and the crudeness of the street, he feels deeply at home in this world. It is divided and antagonistic, filled with human hatreds bred by race, religion and economics; he loves it anyway.

He turns a corner and nearly collides with a regiment of fife and drummers near the Old City Hall. A young man leads it, his fuzzy black Afro powdered white. God stops to watch. What history is being revised or protested on the plaza? Could it be Crispus Attucks, the first man to die in the Boston Massacre of 1770, or one of the famous Fifty-fourth Massachusetts Volunteer Infantry Regiment authorized by President Lincoln in 1863 to fight for the side of the Union? But no, impossible: A bevy of females masses together in the rear of this regiment, backing up the black man like Motown floozies. They whistle shrilly into tin piccolos and drown out the drums. A fantasy history! Who made it up, and why?

The regiment plays "Dying Redcoat" and "Poor Old Tory." A few rheumy veterans with tears in their eyes clasp Red Sox caps to their breasts; God also trembles to the revolutionary music. He has been something of a radical himself, the first Head to find promising colored boys in Roxbury, take them to the Goode School, wake them up and arm them against poverty, drugs and crime with Thomas Hardy and Shakespeare. Integration was *his* cause, his triumph! Now the trustees (Mrs. Rebozos most vocally among them) want to bring girls in.

"Over my dead body," he'd said.

Aileen Rebozos, gamine as she appears, is quite a formidable figure. The first night, he took her to a steak house on the highway, a bit of cowardice he'd assumed he could get away with, as there seemed no question of the thing going anywhere.

"Finish your peas," he reminded her when she lit a cigarette in the middle of dinner; in reply, she poured her drink over his head. God chuckles, recalling aspects of her character that charm him—her direct speech and musculature, her randy infidelity. She and God are foot soldiers, she has informed him, in the sexual revolution. Together with her husband, Viktor, who is for some reason a source of embarrassment, Mrs. Rebozos contributed fifty thousand dollars to save the Goode School from financial exigency, which, Mr. Rebozos lugubriously explained to God, was a form of disease.

"Goode *will* coeducate, just as it has begun to integrate," Mrs. Rebozos pronounced at the last annual meeting. "We will not take no for an answer!"

God had chuckled. *Over my dead body.* Perfectly serious, fair warning—and he'd allowed the moment to pass. It was still unclear to God whether by "we" Aileen Rebozos meant all the women massed behind men and oppressed through the ages, or whether she meant the foot soldiers in the new sexual revolution, of which, she'd assured him, he was also a part, or whether she meant herself and Mr. Rebozos, whose money turned the world.

Then suddenly God is slapped again, jarred from his complacency. He thinks first of his conscience, but no; it's glass. Popping sounds are followed by a blast, then screams, and a few commanding male voices. There's smoke, fire, even laughter—and a rich, almost human scent of burning rubber. He's down on the curb, his arse pecked by little stones. A cold puddle of snow has melted beneath him. A shard of glass sticks out from his forehead, and he flings it from him as if it might explode.

Bomb. The word travels through the air—bomb, a bomb, a bomb blast. Something has blown up. A woman runs down the street directly in front of God, her face closed so tightly, it is not a face. Is it a woman? Her head is anonymous—it could be any head. Instead of hair, it wears a knit woolen cap, blue and green shot through with metallic thread. The figure runs past. Without thinking, an old schoolmaster's instinct, he reaches out for the coattail. The figure—not precisely a "woman," though God can't say why—does not stop or slow. The coat slides down the length of its back, the figure's arms fall to its sides and shed the sleeves. God grips it neatly, his prize.

He has seen revolutionary chaos before, on television: Malcolm X, Huey Newton, Bobby Seale and the Black Panther Party for Self-Defense, Che Guevara, bra-burning women and Ho Chi Minh! A trash receptacle smokes arrogantly on the sidewalk, the metal torn, the trash spilled and burning in the street. It's all part of the spectacle; everyone claims responsibility for destroying the order he loves; everyone has a recipe for an explosive device. A block away, the Irish police move in. Do-gooders rush in toward the trouble. He remembers the red writing on the walls of the bus where he first touched Mrs. Rebozos: *Are we not drawn onward we few drawn onward to new era?* She pointed out that the words spelled the same question backward and forward, a palindrome.

The bomb has carried pieces of him away. There's been a concussion; he is concussed. The angry new women have done it—he has their blue coat as evidence. His ears ring; he can't remember where he put his wagon. Usually, he parks along one of the side streets, or occasionally, and though it pains him, in the paid parking underground. But this afternoon, he can't visualize his car any more than he can see his own face. He finds himself walking along the river, under the bridge. The yellow twilight drains into the dark. He walks until he can't retrace his steps and the only course is forward. Then he walks in darkness, on the side of the highway, breaking laws.

He has never taken a journey like this, alone on foot. Not during the first war, which he spent in Italy. Not during the second war, in China. At the edge of the city, he steps into the fringe: sidewalks, crabgrass, narrow houses with covered porches, the metal detritus of family life—tricycles, charcoal grills. His white face must glow in the dark like a moon. He passes an empty public school, half an acre of macadam surrounded by chain-link fence. A young man brushes by him, whispering, "Smoke, smoke, smoke," and vanishes. God thinks for a moment that he taught this boy in English 6. He continues past empty lots and convenience stores, along a band of gravel. No cars stop; he would not know what to do if they did. His breath steams companionably around his face. Cold rain begins to fall. A pool of yellow light appears, and a sign within the pool reads CHINESE FOOD—COCKTAILS. Behind the sign, a glassed-in room where people eat. In the distance, beyond the restaurant, the skeleton of an old warehouse beckons feebly, bricks and broken windows that God recalls from his youth, the dying days of his grandfather's factory—Byrd Brothers India Rubber. An out-of-date sign on the brick offers the building FOR SALE OR LEASE.

A Chinese woman shows God to a table, where the menu appears under glass. At the adjacent table, four public high school students eat fried egg rolls and play a game of questions. "Ever lose more than fifty dollars on a bet?" "Ever have sex while unconscious?" "Why did thirteen women willingly open their doors to the Boston Strangler?" "Ever been pushed down a flight of stairs by a family member?"

He asks for a bowl of rice. The warm, glutinous grain

together with the chopsticks on the table and the polite offer of the necessary spoon all remind him that he is part of history. He helped to liberate Shanghai!

The revolutionists want to revise history, judge the past by the gleaming standards of the present and kill off old men, men like God. Then the new era will roll out, democratic and diverse. His body buzzes with the same excitement he feels when close to Mrs. Rebozos (the danger, her money and heat). Once again he's the enemy, the target.

God pays for his rice, drapes the fugitive wool coat over the shoulders of his raincoat and marches out into the night, along the postindustrial corridor of Route 8, past the old Byrd Brothers rubber works, which once employed hundreds of men and women in making boots, raincoats, life preservers and, eventually, more delicate female items fabricated and manufactured under his aunt Olympia's supervision. Now only the ghost building survives, followed by an eight-screen cinema and a scrubby, disreputable-looking woods behind the auto mile.

The moon flickers in and out of view. God stumbles on clods of burst tires and cracking ice. Since the navy he hasn't felt so vulnerable or bold. To keep himself company on this strange journey, he works on the memoir he is writing for the Goode School Press, so that future generations might understand what sources nourished the souls of dead white men. Last month, the trustees invited him to retire, to make way for fresh blood. He won't give way until his hour is up, but has been writing in his head for weeks, casting even intimate reflections in polite prose:

> For many years I used to behave badly. We were raised to be moral, but supple. Within certain restrictions—to behave decently in the end—we were perfectly free. We understood that our wives could not be expected to bear the burdens

> that men such as ourselves must impose. I remember meeting my father's mistress, Mrs. Fiske, when I was nine or ten. She had been drinking coffee in the sitting room with my father. I remember their amusement, and my sudden awareness of the circle of people—myself included, and my aunt Olympia and Mrs. Fiske—who contributed to my father's position and well-being. Like my father, I admire youth in a woman—glowing skin, a narrow rack of ribs, milk-bottle arms, sandaled feet, sharp new teeth—

As he walks home, now along the old Post Road toward Cape Wilde, he moves on to larger themes. Cape Wilde is a hard place. Judges used to send girls into exile here rather than bother burning them at the stake, and let Indians take them, or wolves eat them. Sailors have drowned here for centuries; their ships crack up. These days, it's a motif for Sunday painters, who describe the docks and barns and churches whose spires impale the air. There is nowhere God would rather live.

He grew here among other, older Byrds: his father, grandfather, and Olympia, his mother's sister, a radical reformer, an embarrassment and a curiosity; she spent her vital years traveling across New England, campaigning for birth control and the sexual gratification of women. She also advocated for fair working conditions, though she, like God's father, proved mildly oblivious to the anxieties of laboring people. The disposition of family business—the links and chains of history—absorbed them both. They loved nothing better than talking over their investments in an unpretentious restaurant, over cocktails and a cod.

Olympia's arguments poured out in long, uninterruptible loops. There was so much of her to take in—the rich, full-throated voice, her baronial appetite, her extraordinary figure. Her cause consumed her, filled her with a ravenous energy.

When not traveling, she worked in the Byrd Brothers factory, arranging shipments of vulcanized rubber caps to women in Boston and beyond, or inciting halls full of women to demand sexual pleasure. Every word she spoke was charged with passionate intensity about one subject: *Children were avoidable.* Her lectures and demonstrations drew crowds. God's father had once remarked, "People love to listen to your aunt. She has a magnificent bosom."

Olympia sowed one thousand of her caps across five states in the first two decades of the nineteenth century, the way other women massed Dutch bulbs around their birches. Even as a young boy, Goddard was drawn to his aunt, especially in the absence of his mother, who died at eighteen from one of the usual causes—a childbirth infection from a doctor's friendly, filthy hand.

When Goddard turned twelve, his father, concerned that this live-in aunt might exert too strong an influence, took him aside. "Olympia," he explained, "has worked all her life to make sexual union safer for women, so that one day females might undertake congress from healthy desire as much as from duty." (His father's conversation bloomed with legislative metaphors.) Because of Olympia, God always recalled that he'd come himself from a line of revolutionary thinkers and reformers.

As a boy, Goddard studied letters (bound in ribbons) written to Olympia by women whose admiration seemed almost physical in its intensity, as well as intimate objects that moored her to her time and sex: a girdle, a hot-water bottle and siphon, products made possible by Byrd Brothers India Rubber and by his grandfather's work in chemistry, and especially by Charles Goodyear's refinements to latex. Young Goddard occasionally came across Olympia's teeth soaking in a glass of water on her bedside table, resting from their oratorical labors.

He glances up now, across Penzance Point. Has he walked eight miles? He has. (Vitality, longevity!) The moon has risen; water and sky are welded together in glossy black. In the center of the town square, visible from every front-facing window in every house, the original pre-Revolutionary stocks still stand, twin monuments to Cape Wilde's stern views on deviance. The town's civic leaders have since ordered azaleas, lobelia and astilbe to soften extreme impressions left by history. In this season, though, and at night, the square appears austere. God remembers what he must still do. Reread *Heart of Darkness.* Speak up publicly—a letter to the paper? a chapel talk?—about integration and boys. Taste again that roast squab and succotash at the East India House that brought tears to his eyes.

Past midnight, he arrives at his front door (Federal), which is boldly painted red. The house has a date—1732, an old and unimpeachable lie—inscribed on the lintel. God thinks, as he always eventually does, of his wife, of the patient way she bears her impatience, the patina of irritation that brings a glow to her cheek.

She was devoted to him once; he has been, well, faithless. (His forebears were what God's wife calls "rubber barons," but that money has dwindled, and as head of the Goode School, he earns a modest seventeen thousand dollars a year.)

What he reveals now will depend—on her. He'll describe the bomb, the explosion, the confusion, his innocent presence in town. At the proper moment, he will ask for a small glass of gin, which she'll bring to him in a juice glass. Later, she'll make his favorite breakfast—eggs in hell, in a special cup, with Worcestershire. They'll watch the small disaster unfold again on television, listen to the hysterical analysis and exchange their usual remarks. God looks forward to it all. "Home" is a gift presented to him daily by his wife, and God receives such gifts humbly, like alms.

The rubber tree, oppressed these seventy years by the roof, has grown laterally, moving toward the south-facing windows, gracefully bending down and down, its grayish trunk segmented like a worm. The woody fibers where the trunk and branches meet the pointed leaves occasionally crack open and bleed sap down the banister. God's wife, Madeline, stands knifelike at the head of the stairs, one hand resting on the balustrade, the other gripping the pineapple knob. Her attitude is confrontational; her body has become a wall. She has, he sees, been working herself up to this. Her eyes address him with the tense attention of a game animal. (And he is a *tiger*—though a tired old bloody one.)

He will kiss her. Gamely he mounts the stairs, reaches for her pale blue robe. She emits a feral roar and pushes him away with one hand at the center of his chest; the other hand grips the pineapple post. His hands, now empty, grasp at air.

At the cocktail hour, they watch the news on television. Women are enraged about the Miss America pageant, the war and the fascist dictatorship of the nation. Using tactics developed by the Vietcong, they have blown up a trash can in protest, injuring several people. God brings forward the fugitive blue coat as evidence: He was there. Madeline clucks sympathetically but does not, she says, understand him. She sets plates on the table and drops her own bomb. Tonight, after they eat, she will leave him. She stands up straight as a knife in her dowdy town clothes. Her reading glasses hang poised for action in the neck of her jersey; her eyes shine. Her leather handbag on the kitchen counter looks greased and ready to run. A suitcase—from a set that belonged to God's father—stands by the front door.

She gives him a frozen bag of peas to dull the ache in his head, mixes him a drink and pours a small portion for herself. She has been to her GP, come home and packed a bag.

"I had a thorough checkup," she tells him. "It turns out I'm healthier than I thought. Goddard, I could live twenty more years! I drove home and realized how unhappy I am. Twenty more years—I thought I'd have to kill myself.

"This can't surprise you," she tells him, doling out chicken pie and boiled peas. Yet God feels surprised.

"I don't regret my marriage," she says bitterly. "*Je ne regrette rien.*"

"I'm glad of that," he begins.

"I'd like to live for myself. But that's not all. I'm too angry right now to be married to a man like you. You have not been faithful to me. You gave me *crabs.*"

God cannot think how to dignify a remark like this.

"Perhaps you think I'm ridiculous," she says. "But I'm not. Let's not get into the blame game; let's not put labels on each other. You aren't a cad. I'm not a—a *cunt.*"

He finds he can't eat. God puts down his fork and wipes his mouth with a napkin. She has been his amanuensis, his right hand, an efficient machine, deciphering and typing up his pieces for the *Head's Journal,* delivering his opinions to the newspaper. For years she has thrown herself into his work, typing, repairing, introducing new errors and ideas, refinements and subtleties. She helped with his great work to date, a defense of Joseph Conrad, and he dedicated this volume to her: "For my Bride, who kept the home fires burning." She has been useful to him, at least until the middle years, when she sometimes became troubled and drank in the daytime or slept in the garden, or went around the house foaming at the mouth. She pulled out some of her hair, complained of voices in her head. He was, she said then, an exhausting spouse—charming and charismatic, but overbearing, unfaithful and demanding. (She improved somewhat on a diet of witchy-sounding pills, extracted from the urine of a horse.) She might have been an artist (she has that unforgiving temper) but for her tragic flaw—everything she touches turns beautiful. She became, of course, a gardener and rules her dominion like a tyrant. She represses roses and astilbe, withholds water from strawberries, which produce tiny deep red fruit of exquisite intensity. She serves them, in season, at breakfast, in a fluted white bowl. God eats more than his share because she takes less than hers.

She's austere. She prefers the single to the double, the pure marigold to the hybrid that's had the yellow bred out of it, the modest gloxinia to the arrogant giant. Chrysanthemums, yes, dahlias and gladiolus, no. She is devoted to unruffled petunias and her mauve queens. Winters, she reads seed catalogs and leaves lists all over the house—in the telephone book, on the tank of the loo. Names show up like coded messages in the margins of the morning newspaper, folded out to the half-finished crossword: Penn State marigolds, early prolific straight-neck squash, delphiniums, penstemon, butterfly bush, black lilies and fall-blooming rue. He knows all this because she records the little details in a diary, which God occasionally peruses.

His wife could raise a rose from a rake. She throws bleak kindling into a bucket, then calls it a centerpiece—and so it becomes. The sticks leaf out and flower on the piano. She spends whole evenings in the garden, cutting slugs in two and pathologically coaxing nature to an unnatural intensity; she's stuffed forget-me-nots and oxalis in among the ferns.

How can she leave him after all these years? She gives him telephone numbers, instructions on the house and garden, everything he needs written on a lined canary pad.

Now she puts a hand on his arm. God's eyes cloud over and he weeps. He can't stop. She has to sit down awkwardly in a chair, in her coat and gloves, and hold him.

1964 and after

The Strangler

When my father drowned in the ocean off Cape Wilde wearing a pair of Keds sneakers and carrying a dollar in his wallet, the tragedy propelled Mei-Mei and me out of the ordinary even as it sunk us. We were liberated instantly and forever. Life became extraordinary, surreal, unpredictable, and our senses grew acute, like those of wild animals. Mei-Mei, only twenty-nine at the time, fell in love with Tragedy as she had once fallen in love with my father. Tragedy consumed her, wrote his story in lines on her face, comforted her at night with his constancy. Tragedy has been her lover ever since. The story of my father's death was, in this sense, a romance: the story of two bold and irrepressible athletes in a German kayak crossing the eight-mile stretch between Cape Wilde and Capawak Point, a proving ground for generations of Wampanoag braves; the glowering weather on a rainy March afternoon; the dramatic rescue of the other man (by a swimming champion from the public high school); the way the ocean drank my father down and spat him out; the dollar in his pocket when he died.

Mei-Mei has yellowed copies of the newspaper articles from the *Capawak Gazette* and the *Globe* that tell the story. (The reverse of one clipping shows an ad for an outfit that made products out of whalebone: "Ladies Cinched Their Corsets Tight and Danced the Polka in the Mansions of the Nation.") My father's whole life is there in a couple of columns: pitcher on the baseball team in high school and college (he pitched a winning game against Milton Academy the day his father died), almost a year of medical school behind him. Goddard Byrd, head of the Goode School and my father's English teacher, wrote a verse poem called "Anguish and Assuagement," casting Heck Hellman as a heroic athlete in an idealized Greek style:

> Heck, in brief you were too loved to lose
> Bold hero never idle on the field
> We grieve the hour when sport became the ruse
> And life the contest you were forced to yield
> Oceanic depths the cup that holds our tears.

Mei-Mei thought my father's death was a story about accidents, threats, loss, abandonment, risk. "Be careful," she used to tell me when, at fourteen or fifteen, I went out nights in cars with boys. "Don't die," she said.

My first real memories are those years after my father died when Mei-Mei and I used to wait for the Boston Strangler to knock on our door. We waited for night, for the high sound of his car in our driveway, his engine cut, his foot on the stair. We lived in an apartment in one of the old three-story houses near the Four Corners, named for the four corner gas stations that competed there: Esso, Shell, Mobil and another one—Sinclair, now reorganized, or defunct, whose emblem even then was a dinosaur. Most of the houses like ours, once fortresses of the middle class, had become apartment buildings; mostly women lived in them—women with children, women alone. Our apartment occupied the third floor. The rent: $110 a month. The fenced yard kept me near; she wouldn't let me go anywhere without her, afraid someone might steal me.

At night, we ate tiny fried fish with their bones and Mei-Mei played a love song on her guitar—four chords, same song—and

I lay in bed, shimmering with terror because my father was a tiny dead man in the window.

Sometimes I woke up in the dark and couldn't breathe. Mei-Mei turned on the shower and filled the bath with steam. Even now, wasted hot water reminds me of love.

Nobody knew how the Strangler did it. There was no sign of his entering apartments by force. For some reason we didn't understand, the women let him in.

Friday evenings, Mei-Mei and I sat on the twin bed in her room with our backs up against the wall and watched *The Addams Family* on her black-and-white Philco TV. Even though *The Addams Family* was a comedy about a family of ghoulish people—a cousin made of hair, a Thing who was a hand—they didn't fool me. Compared with us, the Addamses were a dream family: extensive, intimate, affluent and serene.

Sometimes a car turned into the driveway. Mei-Mei jumped up from the bed. "Jesus God, who can that be?" She clutched the window frame and stole looks outside. It was always the O'Greefes, who lived downstairs.

Once while I was reading, someone knocked at the front door. I stood up and Mei-Mei ran into the room and knocked me over. She held me down as if I might try to break away. "Who's there?" she called out.

A woman's voice: "I am from the Bureau of the Census."

"We can't let you in," Mei-Mei said. But she let me go. She stood with her mouth up to the closed door, answering the census taker's questions. It looked like whispers and kissing.

The best and most important memories aren't necessarily happy ones; moments of distress sometimes surround moments of bliss. When I cried over some large or small humiliation, Mei-Mei never said "Shh," or "Everything is going to be all right." She just let me lie in her arms in the yellow light from the paper lantern above her bed.

Mei-Mei loves other people's tragedies: She defends their

sad stories; no detail is too shocking or personal. Before she took over the French classes, the previous teacher having been fired for moral turpitude following a sex scandal, Mei-Mei used to teach English literature at Wilde High. Every year she read *The Scarlet Letter* with her students and told them the story of our very own Hester Prynne, Mrs. O'Greefe, whose husband abused her. (He once bit off part of her breast.) Mei-Mei taught her students about the symbolism of what Mrs. O'Greefe had done. (She had had her own nipple grafted onto her forehead.) For Mei-Mei, Mrs. O'Greefe was a hero, a sensual woman trapped in the purlieus of Cape Wilde who turned her oppression by forces of stupidity, poverty and violence into a badge of honor, or at least into a badge.

Once, Mei-Mei made a cake that exploded, and a spray of chocolate stuck to the ceiling forever. Our fear, too, was a mark that never disappeared, even when the Strangler confessed and went to prison, where he was assassinated; even when we moved. It's all still vivid, the chocolate on the ceiling and the cozy nightmare Mei-Mei and I shared. During the commercials, we remembered how the Strangler murdered women with their own bathrobe cords and their own nylons tied in terrible bow ties around their necks. We would keep him out; we would never let him in. Our life was almost like a game. Before we went to bed, we stood empty bourbon and milk bottles in front of the door, then waited in the night to hear glass break.

1968

The Seducer

God despised the telephone, and had no choice but to use the thing. He shouted down the wire to Heck Hellman's widow, "Better come by Thursday afternoon and have a drink."

He had no doubt she'd come when he called, appear at his civilized house on Cape Wilde. Women craved luxury. They were curious and liked to talk. Her husband, Heck, had been one of the great Goode boys—not a scholar particularly, but a first-rate athlete. He'd died five years ago in a boating accident. She never remarried, a tragedy; finally, God had thought of a way to help her.

Looking forward to the appointment, he bathed and deployed bay rum. He put on khaki pants, a striped shirt and a bow tie, feeling like Marlow among the cannibals, not wanting to appear unappetizing. He drove to Maidenhead for a bottle of gin—a necessary trip from dry Cape Wilde. He made ice.

By early afternoon, God lay in his chair, eyes closed, reviewing his position. It pained him to be dismissed as a moth-eaten conservative, an antifemale chauvinist, a reactionary fogy. But he drew the line at girls at Goode, had opposed them to the end. "Over my dead body"—he may have said it two or three times.

Goode had begun as a seminary to train ministers—the grandsons of rebels from the Church of England—in a time when this goal represented an ideal neither diverse nor ecumenical. (We are all, God felt, children of some revolution.) Coeducation was not simply a problem of *including girls,* whatever that idea could come to mean; it was the other language—about *creating a more socially and culturally relevant curriculum*—that troubled him. What did the school stand for, after all, but a certain kind of boy—who presented himself to God's imagination in the image of Heck Hellman or Archer Rebozos—whose character was forged on the playing field, whose soul was enlarged (but not falsely puffed up) by literature and language, whose mind was sharpened by mathematics and science, whose spirit was tuned by daily hours in chapel to the profound mysteries of life, whose manners at table were stiffened like lightly starched napkins by years of French service at the evening meal? Even if on the surface God's boys resembled regular boys of the era, with their long hair and woozy airs, they were at heart conservative in the Goode School tradition—boys in possession of traditions worth conserving.

Still, Postover and Mellon-Hardgraves had brought girls in. The new, mercenary board of trustees naturally feared females straying into the boys' rooms—and worse—but had already made the fatal financial decision. Times were changing. Goode was like the besieged South Vietnamese city of Ben Tre: It had become necessary to destroy the school in order to save it.

Heck Hellman's wife appeared at five in a skirt and tall boots. She stood under the wisteria vine that had devoured and become the pillars of the porch: beaky nose, upright bosom, untamed brown mane. "Call me Mei-Mei," she said, and stuck out her hand to shake. Her fresh aspect under the hoary branches reminded him that even as he prepared to step aside—the call for "mandatory retirement" at sixty-five still rang in his ears—new grass had grown under his feet. He would show them, take a bold last stand; he would call his work *In Defense of Boys: A Last Stand Against the Adoption of Coeducation at the Goode School.* He only really needed someone to type it.

"Come in," he said. "Give me your sweater. Sit down."

He mistrusted her enough that he became, if anything, more courtly. "I want to offer you a special cocktail—the world's oldest soft drink—a *sha-rub*."

They went together to the kitchen. He located glasses, and the raspberry syrup, the vinegar mix, the fizzy water. He made a production.

"Arabic," she said.

"I'm afraid I'm a bit of an Orientalist. Splash of gin?"

"Oh, yes."

He told a few self-deprecating stories, including a hint of why his wife had left him—unbridled vitality!—then pulled back. He laid his hands down on the table in front of him, looked meditatively at the veins.

"Heck was one of the great boys of Goode," he said. "I remember him perfectly, an epitome." His eyes misted over, speaking of the old days, the old boys, Heck. "I did not invent the form," he told Mei-Mei, "though I may have played some part in perfecting the model."

This was part of what he hoped to show in his book. "Did I tell you the name of it? *In Defense of Boys*." He described the models he'd built on, the boys he'd turned out, the men he had helped to forge in the smithy of his school. More than that, he was uniquely positioned to give a history of the century, with which he had almost perfectly coexisted—the who, what, when, where and why—a history that might otherwise be lost.

"It is, among other things, a story about formidable women," he assured her. His first memory as a boy was of sitting under the piano on a Persian rug in short pants, and the rug scratching his knees. His aunt Olympia swept into the room wearing a broad, complicated hat; her eye slid over him. Summers, his father let him go out alone along the shores of Squantum, first in a dory, then in his own twelve-foot sloop. Aunt Olympia saved his life once when he swamped: She swam to him and hauled him home. He remembered rhododendrons, peonies, boatyard rats, slipping into the cinema and spending his Sunday nickel for church. Then school: He was sent away and wet his bed. The mattress was publicly aired. The first Negro pupil, Ames, had a gold tooth and brought his girl to a dance one time. Up until then, everyone admired a man on his merits, no matter his race. But they could not bring themselves to admit the couple into their circle, and Ames left the dance with a cold air. God did not speak up at the time, and the incident shamed him.

He felt now, more than ever, a compulsion to communicate, and dreaded the loss of voice that death might bring.

"What's this music?" Mei-Mei asked.

"Verdi's Requiem," he told her. "Memory of Heck."

"It's just loud—the trumpets."

She stood up, crossed the living room and turned down the music. She came back and sat beside him. Beneath the tidy line of her skirt, her knees did not quite touch. "I'd like to help you, Mr. Byrd," she said. "I can type sixty-five words a minute."

Their work began well; Mei-Mei seemed charmed by the Underwood in the bonny nook upstairs, content in God's realm. She had another job, teaching English in the local high school, and came to him in the early evenings and on weekends. Sometimes after she transcribed a section of his notes, he would feed her a glass of gin and listen to her talk. "Heck and I made love the night before he died. When I heard he'd drowned, I couldn't see my life anymore. It just went dim. I hoped I was pregnant. And I prayed—prayed!—I was not. I couldn't sleep, the conflict of these two desires was so intense. I have never wanted—and not wanted—anything so much since then."

God was relieved to hear her speak frankly of desire. When he eventually revealed himself, she was not instantly repelled, and he felt grateful for those aspects of women that he found so admirable: their courtesy and almost natural ability to minimize the discomfort and awkwardness of being old bones in a body. He peeled away his khaki pants and shorts, revealed his rotund paunch, his sagging thighs, his full preparedness for engagement (!) even as he acknowledged to himself a minor note of disappointment (how many torch songs raveled out on that minor note?) that she had been so easy a summit to conquer. The thought didn't shame him—why should it? He had no reason to worry about any invasion of the private sphere of his mind (because his mind was like a First World nation—protected, defended), and lascivious thoughts ran like gold through the gutters. He was grateful that she showed no sign of being repelled by his aged carcass, and only mildly sorry that she was not just slightly younger, in a tighter stage of bud.

"Well?" he said. "Shall we put it in?"

"I want you to," she said tragically.

They fucked in silence on the Persian gabbeh in the bonny nook. Mei-Mei came, then God.

Mei-Mei wept; she typed. She typed all night and words came out. She had to tell Heck's story; she wrote. "Every sentence must be just so," God had said, "before you can go on." He was important; she typed. Every sentence must be just so; she wept. She made the imperfect sentences disappear, until nothing remained and the story—his story (also in some important way *her* story)—was like perfect sentences written in milk on a white page: not a shadow of the story, but a page too white to read. In this way, she tried to create by deleting, making the man come alive even as he receded and dissolved.

Mei-Mei proved to be a distracted amanuensis—and a liar about her typing skills. A professor in college had advised her not to learn, she confessed, as a sort of prophylaxis against becoming a secretary. Mrs. Graves, less tragic and snobbish and more tractable, who opposed girls and sat directly behind God in the hallway of the castle where he commanded his post, absorbed his notes into her general duties.

But God kept Mei-Mei on. In memory of Heck Hellman, he helped her as he could.

1969

God-Father

EV, nearly nine, knows she can win God over if she tries. He sits at the kitchen table, smoking, a Pall Mall in one hand and a red pencil in the other. He smokes and then blows out his cheeks; he rocks back and forth in his chair as he reads, talking to himself in a low voice. Sometimes he ejaculates "Ha!" or "Hup!" His red pencil idles above a page, which trembles slightly, as if in terror. Mei-Mei stands at the kitchen counter holding a cup of coffee.

"What's so funny?" she asks him.

"Essay on *Lear.* Well done. Wish I could write half as well. Hup!"

Mei-Mei reaches behind herself and unties her apron. "What mark are you going to give it?" She hangs the apron on a nail in the cellar door, then takes her cup to the sink, where she washes her lipstick from the lip. EV makes a note: Women put things on—aprons and lipstick—then take them off.

"Eighty-nine," God says, and writes the number on the top of the page in red. It's the first girl's first paper. He'd do the same for anyone.

God stirs martinis in a porcelain bucket called "the urinal." EV has studied what he gets from gin. His face relaxes; his icy eyes soften. He forgets and remembers things. Sometimes he puts a Mabel Mercer or a Fats Waller record on the turntable and sits with his hands on the arms of his yellow chair while his eyes fill up. Or he plays the piano wildly by ear, translating lyrics into animal grunts. His hands move like claws across the keys, the fingers bent to attack the chords. His glass on the edge of the piano bursts into beads of sweat from the heat of it. He never takes his hands from the keys or a sip from his glass when he plays. His drink consumes itself and he wants more.

EV sits on the rug on the floor, watching his foot on the brass pedals, the shifting legs of his khaki pants. She wishes she could just live in his body, wear his pants, shirts and tweedy jackets on her own skin. But her clothes—jumpers and white blouses with Peter Pan collars—come from the daughter of a friend of Mei-Mei's who is always older and larger than EV.

God's head appears under the piano: "You might bring me a glass of the ice water." After two drinks, what's left at the bottom of the urinal is called "ice water."

It's important that Mei-Mei not see EV, who waits under the piano for a sign, Mei-Mei closing the door to the toilet, or her unhappy hum flowing into a remote region of the house. Then she climbs the cellar stairs, collects the watery dregs from the urinal and returns to him with the treasure. He pretends not to see it; he pretends not to care.

Too much to drink and he simply goes to bed. EV wants him just soft enough to notice small things—herself, for example. She wishes he would teach her. In a way he does teach her, and in this way she learns everything.

After dinner—baked fish, snipped green beans—EV says to Mei-Mei, "Tickle me." She's already itchy with anxiety, interested in the extreme margins of feeling—pleasure, agony, distress, bliss. God says he finds it perverse for an almost-nine-year-old to be unnaturally interested in these things, although Mei-Mei assures him that many almost-nine-year-olds *are* interested.

He reads *Heart of Darkness* at the kitchen table. He's an old man already, fat in the middle, pink-headed and jowly; EV prefers him.

She brushes her teeth while Mei-Mei makes the bed perfect, wipes the sheet with her hand and erases the lines, punches the pillow and sets it upright. She pulls back the wool blanket in a triangle like the flap of an envelope, and EV slides inside like a letter.

Not everyone likes children; EV herself does not like them. Mei-Mei reads a few pages from a story about a woman who turns into a dog. She reads fluently, not really listening to the words. EV's attention is divided, too, part of it held by the story, the woman turning into a dog, and part watching the dark parts of Mei-Mei's eyes flit back and forth.

When Mei-Mei finishes the story, she kisses EV on the cheek and turns out the light. "I know what you're up to," she says from the doorway. "I suppose you can't help it, but I don't like it."

The bed is warm and the sheets are clean. EV shudders with animal pleasure.

For the rest of our lives, Mei-Mei remembered things differently.

"God wasn't your father!" she said, horrified. "We didn't marry him, darling. We stayed with him in a difficult period. My husband had died, for Christ's sake! Russian missiles in Cuba were pointed at Boston! The president was assassinated! And we were poor, poor! And God's wife had left him."

"But we lived there," I reminded her. "I slept in the bonny nook."

"We lived there for a month, two months."

"You and God were lovers."

Mei-Mei wrinkled her nose. "I wouldn't call it *that*."

"What would you call it?"

"Sometimes I was lonely. But it turned out that with God I was lonelier."

Mei-Mei and I lived in so many different places. I remembered parts of all of them—the horrible apartment on Eden Court above the O'Greefes', where we waited for the Strangler to tie his bows around our necks. Then one summer the Fiskes went to France and we stayed at their farmhouse in Squantum; then we rented a detached basement on Penzance Road. We house-sat for Mrs. Graves from the Goode School while she went to Reno for her divorce; then Mei-Mei inherited Madame Bonnard's French class and we bought the house in Maidenhead.

But I remember God's house as if my life happened there, as if it were my house. I sifted through the pennies and the rolls of Tums on his bureau, examined his artifacts: the shaving brush and bowl, the Zippo lighter, the red pencils and hand sharpeners in the drawers of his black India-rubber desk, the row of khaki pants and hanging shirts and crumbly wool jackets in his closet and, toward the back, an old blue coat made of cheap wool, serge, with brass buttons, obviously not a coat that he would ever wear—too small, too effeminate, too cheap. I put this coat on and wore it everywhere, waiting for him to acknowledge my audacity. One day he looked up and saw me finally. "Ha! Hup!" he said, and that was all. In the coat I felt most like myself—ironic, disguised, dangerous. What girl of some ambition does not in her formative years wear a coat two sizes too large for her? When Mei-Mei and I left God's house, he gave me the coat to keep; at least I took it with me.

1969

The First Girl

A few brown and black faces swam in the sea of white boys at Goode, and several female faculty had penetrated, but Carole was the only *girl,* a misunderstanding that arose from a clerical error when Mrs. Graves, distracted by her embarrassing and ultimately liberating divorce, mistakenly included Carole's name in the "Negro" acceptance pool under the traditional male name Carroll. (The school had interviewed a few girls and international students for admission, but God had prevailed upon the trustees to stay coeducation for one more year.) By the time Mrs. Graves discovered her error, Carole had already received and accepted her guarantee-of-scholarship letter; she had, indeed, already arrived.

On the first day of the first girl, Carole, fifteen, entered the classroom in advance of God, whose tweedy arm held the door, his patrician fingers spread expressively across the oak. The second-year boys looked up from their Arden Shakespeares, their *Lear.* As a group, the twenty boys gave off an impression of slightly fetid humidity, limp bangs, cotton shirts. Carole, too, might have seemed to the boys at that moment unspecific as she stumbled (or was pushed) over the doorjamb and appeared as a synecdoche, embodying blackness exponentially intensified by gender.

"*Gentlemen!*" said God, whose final, often-quoted statement on the subject of girls—"over my dead body"—still hung in the air. The boys rose; the wood floor groaned. Carole stood in the door, blocking God, who pinched the sleeve of her boy's blue blazer and moved her out of his way so that he could command this historic moment and properly introduce her.

She was tall and slim as a boy, with caramel-colored skin and reddish hair that framed her face in a fuzzy halo. She wore pants, a printed blouse and the blazer, flat shoes. (Who knew then about mandatory skirts for girls, as there were no rules, as there were no girls?)

Everyone examined her as God spoke ecumenically, if a little muddily, about Crispus Attucks, the first man to die in the Boston Massacre of 1770, about the famous Negro regiment, the Fifty-fourth Massachusetts. He spoke of the liberalism of Greeks, the tolerance of the Founding Fathers, the end of slavery and the eventual enfranchisement of all men—and women. He remembered Jackie Robinson joining the Brooklyn Dodgers in 1947 and ending the segregation of players in the Negro leagues. He veered back to the Enlightenment and Rousseau. He spoke of Frederick Douglass, Joe Louis, Paul Robeson, W. E. B. DuBois and Malcolm X, who, in his formative years, had worked as a busboy at the Parker House Hotel! He wound up with the late Reverend Martin Luther King, Jr. (here God's eyes filled with tears), who'd had a dream of equality that was even now being realized at Goode. When he finished, it seemed the air itself might detonate from the pressure.

God turned his back on the class and wrote slowly in chalk on the blackboard, "Are we not drawn onward we few drawn onward to new era?"

He laid the chalk in the tray, turned and held out a hand for Carole Faust to shake. "Welcome to the Goode School at the dawn of a new era," he said. "I trust you will acquit yourself modestly and be a credit to—and be a credit to the institution."

Her hand literally crackled when he shook it, as if a bone had broken. "I might be a little tense," Carole said.

The boys erupted in sympathetic laughter and burst into applause. Wasn't everyone a little tense?

Mrs. Graves addressed the problem of Carole—which God perceived as a women's problem—by grouping her with the international boys, who came from Paris, Cairo, Hyderabad and Frankfurt. All the "different" students, she reasoned, would feel more comfortable together. She resolved the question of propriety by putting one of the unmarried female faculty (Julia Singer, Art Department) in charge of International House.

After the first dinner, which Carole ate with the international boys, she went into the courtyard, where some upperformers were handing around a package of Winstons. Carole pulled out her own pack—of Kools. "The ghetto cigarette," she told them.

Out of respect, the boys called her by her surname, as if she were one of them. She was never Carole, only Faust. But she was not one of anything; she was singular. Because of her, girls had to be brought in at the second semester. Because of Carole, the whole world changed.

In her first year, Carole watched, adapted and generally did what one might expect of a teenager. She took some pains to differentiate, to assert and accentuate her otherness, which God and Mrs. Graves found perverse. (Goode was already integrated, God insisted—23 of the 370 students were Negro—but still Carole chose to wear her difference, her blackness and femaleness, like a banner.) The Rebozos family—Aileen Rebozos was a trustee—had taken a special interest in Carole, who had spent part of the previous summer with the Rebozos family on Capawak Island. The Rebozoses had somehow found Carole in Brooklyn, New York—the bright daughter of an ambitious immigrant from the West Indies, some old family connection.

When Carole returned in the fall, she refused to read the book that every Goode student read. Why would she not read the book that every student read? asked God. Because it bored her. And how could this book, which contained all the seeds of humanity, *Heart of Darkness, bore* her? It just did. She liked some other books by white men—for example, *Moby-Dick*. A book about a whale—a book that took on the separateness of a species. "If only someone would acknowledge that 'some of us' are whales!" "Whales?" "Yes, fearful symbols."

"And what are you a symbol of?" asked God.

"I just said. Of your fear."

She was supported in her rebellion by some of the female faculty—Julia Singer in particular—and by many of the boys, black and white, and even by the new girls, who had no basis to complain. *The Goodeman* ran a front-page photograph showing the awful rally of protest, students carrying crude placards that read ANGRY BLACK WHALE, WHITE WHALE and SPERM WHALE and WHO IS MOBY-DICK?

It was, finally, her stance, hands on hips, her face, the placid look, when he was accustomed (from the boys, from everyone but his wife) to slightly glazed expressions of admiration. God's famous equipoise suddenly cracked open like an egg.

"What makes you think you know what art is? What makes you so sure that you know what is real and what is false, what is good and what is not? *What makes you think you know the answers?*"

She just knew, she said, and she knew what she knew. She didn't remember a time not knowing. She flunked chemistry; she never turned in her final paper on the *Odyssey* because, it turned out, she was interested only in the *idea* of the book, the hero's journey; she couldn't actually read it; she couldn't, actually, stand it.

"It takes discipline to be a scholar," God thundered to Mrs. Graves. "It even takes discipline to be an artist. Who the hell does she think she is?"

"Carole lacks discipline; she is casual and loose," God wrote to the mother, Mrs. Faust, in a letter of probation he dictated to Mrs. Graves, who typed furiously.

As more girls and more students of color arrived, it became clear that the issues of integration and coeducation were not only about ethnicity and gender but also about class and culture. In time, the chapel became a "cultural center"; Father Reiss was released from his part-time duties. Carole herself, who seemed to embody blackness, oppression, sexism, equal opportunity and "religious tolerance"—a muddy commingling of any faith that anyone suggested—grew tired of representing these ideas, tired of masters habitually tilting in her direction when they mentioned slavery or civil rights, a long history of racist and sexist assumptions burning brightly in their apologetic eyes.

In her second year, instead of entering into the traditions of the school with an open, humble mind, Carole created a spectacle in the back of the field bus—beyond the purview of the rearview, Mrs. Graves told God drily. Kissing boys was one thing—the school had prepared for that eventuality. But a girl kissing another girl, in the bus, in front of the boys—on the way to Lake Winnipesaukee! These girls were not innocents, Mrs. Graves assured him. They understood power and seduction and manipulated boys who'd been, let's face it, pretty protected.

"She likes girls?" God asked, incredulous.

"Evidently," said Mrs. Graves, "as she is kissing them."

"Then what did she come to a boys' school for?"

"I'll ask her."

Mrs. Graves unfolded her half-glasses, slid them on her face and read, "The girls made a bet with each other—a dare. A dare to kiss. Tongues were used." Mrs. Graves read the passive construction with distaste, then looked up. "Is this correct?"

Carole looked away, smiling slightly.

"This is neither a racial nor a sexual issue, Carole; this is a point of character. You are sabotaging yourselves. You are sabotaging this beautiful revolution. Don't you realize how fortunate you are?"

Carole shrugged.

"Coeducation—it was not just for you. It was for all of us who dream of equality for women, equality for all people. Have you read the school's policy on diversity and inclusion?"

"No," said Carole.

"Well, it is a beautiful statement—a beautiful idea. I hate it that you did this *to yourself,* Carole," Mrs. Graves said. Her hands wound around each other. Carole said nothing, the sleeves of her boy's undershirt peeled up over her shoulders like a sneer.

"After so many people have been so kind to you. The Rebozos family, for example. They have been tremendous, Carole—tremendously kind."

Carole said nothing.

"Do you envy the boys, dear?" Mrs. Graves asked gently. "Is that why you're dragging yourself down?"

"Who wouldn't envy the boys?" Carole asked.

After she sent Carole Faust away, Mrs. Graves ate an apple at her desk. She felt strong and clear, like the time after her divorce a year ago, when she lived alone in the big house she'd won in the settlement, with the bathroom chests full of pharmaceuticals from her ex-husband's company, and her ex-husband's gun. A rabid skunk had come around and lived under the house for three days, foaming and threatening her safety and peace, the white stripe down the back of the black animal bristling and quivering. Instead of becoming hysterical or calling a man or taking pills, she calmly stood on the porch and shot the miserable thing.

"By the twenty-four testicles of the twelve apostles of Christ," God remarked to Mei-Mei as he stirred gin into the urinal. "What do women want? Women on the syllabus when they haven't read what's *on* the syllabus. Birth-control pills! Hup! They want to be lesbians! They don't know what they want; they're ungrateful, hostile and sexed-up. We have been *notoriously* liberal and fair-minded. The boys all read Rousseau's 'Discourse on the Origin and the Foundation of the Inequality Among Mankind' in ninth grade!"

"And the girls," I said.

"What's that?" said God, who had trouble hearing female voices.

"The boys and the girls. Everyone reads it."

"So they do," said God.

"If *you* don't lead the way, who will?" said Mei-Mei. "Did you read that book by the teacher who was fired for reading a Langston Hughes poem to his students in Roxbury?"

God's eyes lit up. "Kozol! I taught him English," he said.

"Exactly. If you aren't out front on attacking inequity and segregation, who will be?"

God sipped his drink, puffed up a little.

"Besides, who isn't ungrateful, hostile and sexed-up? It's like a viral infection."

"Hup."

I knew Carole Faust from God's stories; I think I remember every word he ever said about her, every chapter from their existential agon. God and Carole were opposites, drawn to each other for the purpose of some struggle that took place almost before my eyes and formed my consciousness. (I wanted to be him, and wanted to be her.) I was nine her first year—the year of the first girl—and ten her second year, when Carole was sixteen. But I never met her in person until much later, long after we'd left God's house, when Mei-Mei and I attended her final project, an answer to the question posed to every senior at Goode: "Is the history of mankind a relentless search for freedom?" Her answer was a series of portrait paintings of the fourteen heads of the school, from 1827 down to the present—fourteen men in high middle age—ending with Goddard Byrd. Carole painted them formally, under the direction of Julia Singer. In the absence of a studio art department—the school emphasized history, though it maintained a potter's wheel for troubled boys—Carole set up paints and an easel in a disused alcove in the basement near the girls' bathroom.

She painted from old etchings, drawings or photographs, with particular, almost obsessive attention to their facial features—beaks, brows and jowls. Because God was, in contrast to her other subjects, alive, she'd gone to his office one afternoon in the fall of her senior year to take his picture herself. She loosened him up by asking questions: "What's your favorite animal, Mr. Byrd?" (A tiger.) "Favorite vegetable?" (Corn on the cob.) She encouraged him to recite poetry—Shakespeare's sonnets, that John Masefield chestnut about the seas. I imagined how he would become more real, reciting. Before Carole began painting a week later, she showed him the photograph—God at his desk, his watery blue eyes scanning the playing fields, his mouth pensively ajar—which he approved.

She mounted her portrait series at a regular Friday-evening soirée in the castle, an event that also featured a musician named Ray—a prodigy God had plucked himself from Roxbury—who played a Bach cello suite entitled "Falling Down Stairs." There was also a symposium on "The Goode School Experience from the Perspective of the Black Day Boy," organized by God himself in response to statistical reports that boarders earned better grades, liked school more and were substantially more likely to contribute to the annual fund in the future than those who lived at home. At the last minute, the air filled with static—faculty, girls and students of color objected to the word *boy*. Ms. Inge, who taught American History, proposed that everyone correct "her or his" programs to read "students."

"What's this?" God asked, his eyes glittering. "In what kind of a school is a head not permitted to use the word *boy*?" His words hung in the air of the chilly castle (imported brick by brick from Scotland by Dick Whitehead, '18) while God looked around the Great Hall and waited for someone to agree with him.

In the second part of the evening, Julia Singer stepped forward and introduced Carole Faust and her project: "The Venerable Heads."

Carole wore blue jeans—against the rules, even for boys—and a tight green military jacket. She remained in the back of the room with her slide projector, even after applause called her forward.

"In my first year at Goode," Carole began, "I tried to fit in, excel and follow the path described to me by my mother and by all the adults around me as the path toward freedom. My mother—who can't be with us tonight because she works a minimum-wage job with no protections and doesn't own a car—is an exceptionally strong-willed person, and for a long time I thought I wanted what she wanted. Here at Goode, I began to see freedom as the actual opposition to racist and sexist oppression, although the subject of 'freedom' begs the question of who is 'free' and at what cost—and includes the whole history of oppression and the whole history of the oppressor. Instead of coming to Goode and learning to identify with the oppressor and gain freedom that way, I've come to define myself *by* my difference and otherness—inhabit and *suffer* it in the sense of the Latin root, meaning 'to endure.' To suffer includes the act of bearing suffering; it's a form of transcendence and action. In the same way, I've chosen to take power over my art by painting only the Other—the white, the male, the symbols of oppression to me personally and to the culture as a whole.

"My project," Carole went on, "is called 'The Venerable Heads.' It's a series of portraits exploring representations of the venerable. What do we venerate and what does the object of our veneration have in common with what we have venerated before? What signals the presence of authority and power? In traditional portraiture, the subject presents the face of his venerability. He's depicted with his special finery, against a backdrop that serves as evidence of his wealth or position. In this slide, Gilbert Stuart's 'unfinished' portrait of George Washington suggests through unpainted canvas that Washington, the figure, the character, is not yet 'finished' or sealed by history. The impression of humanity, or progress of the individual, is in this way heightened." She ran through some slides of seventeenth-century Dutchmen and portraits by John Singleton Copley, showing men posed with their dogs and tools. "In more contemporary work," she went on, "portraits consolidate social, moral, political or economic influence—heads of state or heads of corporations or organizations. The subject is made as static as possible to convey the impression of stability and solidity, as much as these impressions can be conveyed by a head.

"I've tried, for my senior project, to learn these techniques of the patriarchy, so that I can subvert them in my own work."

She walked along the exhibition wall and pulled away the black cloths that covered six of the heads, each rendered in a yearbook-style black and white, except for some canny work she had done with the eyes, every pair a different color—blue, green, brown, yellow, gray and red. Finally, she unveiled God's portrait as head of the school. It met with silence, followed by a yelp of laughter. A classical portrait, it lacked any of the usual fastenings—chest, shoulders, neck. The head simply rested on the bottom of the canvas, and offered a likeness that slightly flattered its subject.

"What a shame," said Mrs. Graves. "It would have been lovely to hang these in the hall."

"It *would* be fascinating to actually hang them," said Ms. Bruns, who taught drama. "Something interesting to look at and provocative to think about."

"Carole is a gifted painter, and, more important, her work challenges *consciousness,*" Julia Singer said.

A hand shot up. "If you are interested in black power, Carole, why didn't you invent an Afro-feminist way of painting, rather than reusing and perverting the traditional, European portrait techniques?"

"The European canon is all I know," Carole said.

"But how can you love the form if you hate the history?"

"I don't know. It's a problem."

"But you're part *of* it—the history. Don't you see? Isn't it exciting to be among the very first class of girls?"

"Yes," said Carole.

During the reception, Carole and several accomplices pulled the portraits off the walls and took them into the quadrangle and set them on fire.

Carole later claimed that the fire was part of the project—an investigation of authorship and authority, the ultimate freedom of the creator, ending in "a heap of burning images." She wrote the required apology, but in it she claimed her work had been "censured." No one came strongly to her defense. Her mother wrote a letter of apology to *The Goodeman,* offering to pay for any damage. But the damage was done, God's face blackened, smeared and burned away around one ear.

For years after, Carole worked only on painted heads, sometimes white and sometimes black, always male, always moved to the very edge of the canvas. Each of them was titled *Self-Portrait:*

Self-Portrait with Navy Hat, Self-Portrait with Apocalypse, Self-Portrait with Swimming Pool, Self-Portrait with Dog. The paintings didn't usually include the promised artifacts—the hat, the apocalypse, the swimming pool, the dog. They were just heads, no necks. They looked like bowling balls, decapitations. They looked as if they had rolled there.

1973

The Greedy Girl

Church was exciting—Father Reiss admitted he'd hit on one of the girls from confirmation class—but EV's stomach rumbled through it all. Newly confirmed herself, she'd run five miles before breakfast, and thought fiercely of the sandwiches.

She knelt, she stood, she sang and then she finally sat in the midsection of St. Vitus while the minister resigned. Father Reiss was not a crapulous old moralist in a robe—he looked like a movie star. He had an elongated owl's head, live eyes and red lips. The story of his fall was widely, almost omnisciently known: It had happened one afternoon when his wife knocked on the door to the rector's office, then opened it to ask Father Reiss whether he minded olives in a sauce on his spaghetti. She found him pressed into the tapestry couch, on top of some girl from Cape Wilde.

EV had been there herself with Father Reiss a year ago, before her confirmation—a willing victim, a seducer. For as long as she could remember (nine?) she'd tried to rub the gloss of innocence *off* in the same way she'd washed her new blue jeans with stones to remove their embarrassing freshness, their starch. "You are such a puppy," Father Reiss had said in a baby voice. "You have legs like a boy." His face hung on her, his mouth glittered and EV's eye drifted. It can be hard to hear a compliment, or even read one on a lover's lips—and the fever of his passion was ultimately too adult, and boring.

Now Father Reiss held a ballpoint pen in one hand as he read from the apology he'd prepared in the study that was the scene of his crime. He popped the point in and out, in and out, like a pulse.

> Good morning, everyone. I stand before you today as an example, a negative example, as a reminder of human frailty, as a warning. Many of you in this room are my friends. Many of you have come to me for guidance through the trials of your lives, for succor in your sorrow. You have invited me to witness, confirm and partake in your joys. You have trusted me to hold the cord that binds this community to one another and to God. I stand here today having violated that trust. . . .

The congregation listened sympathetically. They'd lost three ministers in three years (one to divorce, one to cancer). Father Reiss possessed a unique, if excessive, charm and had been diplomatic in managing the choir, not like the last one—a music snob who came up from the city and purged the tenors. Father Reiss had been the chaplain at the Goode School until integration and coeducation collided explosively into a new condition called "diversity," the chapel was turned into an ecumenical cultural center and moral guidance became a function of the Office of Student Health. No one ever complained or missed him, with the exception of one student, Carole Faust, who, in spite of her rage against the patriarchy and the fact that her people were evangelical, had come down every Sunday while at Goode to sing in the choir.

Through some feat of fortitude for which they might have trained all their lives, Father Reiss's wife and daughter sat in the second pew, buttresses for the sagging soul at the pulpit. At the end of his speech, Father Reiss lifted his beautiful face to confront his accusers. Who had accused him? the congregation wondered. Had he accused himself? The molested child had defiantly not accused him, had refused.

"Let us pray," he said.

Everyone but Father Reiss himself knelt down, relieved. His wife and daughter knelt on their velvet hassocks and hung their heads, raising the brows of brown hair that ran across the backs of their mother-daughter cable-stitched cardigans.

The mother had sharper edges and tight cords in her neck. The daughter, who was ten or eleven, looked softer and looser. EV touched the sketchbook in her bag. She'd like to draw these two as they stood or prayed. Would anyone care? (The congregation kept busy kneeling, standing, sitting.)

A bright scent of mothballs hung in the church, and dust from fifty women's hats drifted in slow motes across the lavender light from the Tiffany window that revealed the last temptation of Christ.

EV knelt on her hassock to pray: *Spare me the shapeless waiting of girls to be confirmed or otherwise awakened.* Sometimes this year she felt so *hot,* nothing but a temptation, even to herself; she glowed, nerve endings clenched with sudden agony or shrill delight.

EV's sympathies were, of course, all with Father Reiss. She understood lust, deceit, perversity, gluttony, curiosity. He'd gone too far; he'd helped himself. EV admired that. Go too far, get caught and take the others with you into the thick of it, smile into the bright eyes and the lights, say, "Yes, I did it," force them all to react. Who knew better than Father Reiss how much the parish needed to forgive? These dry souls in their cardigans and hats and blazers hoped—they prayed—that any lapse within their imagination could be cured by a fifty-minute hour of easy worship. (As a precaution, they had Father Reiss in for strong drinks twice a year and stuffed him full of salty hors d'oeuvres.)

She would be different, renounce faith and family, publish

the secrets, sleep with the enemy. Ha! She'd break some serious rule, then wait—as Father Reiss waited now—to see what would happen.

EV rubbed her hands together to warm them, then pulled out her sketchbook, her charcoal pencil. She drew mother and daughter Reiss—Jeanne and Ruby—their bland, oblivious backs, the shoulder blades under the cardigans just visible, like folded wings. She began an intricate rendering of the cardigans' cable pattern, then finished it off quickly with a pattern of *x*'s and *o*'s. The abrasive scratch on paper was magnified slightly by the cavern of the nave; she might have been rubbing a scabbed knee. She turned the page and drew Father Reiss at the pulpit, his difficult face. She drew the ball of tissue in his hand, the hand that held the tissue. (Had he been crying? The wimp!) But she caught something there. She recalled dry legs, her itchy jumper, Father Reiss's cool, damp hands; she excelled at hands.

The Episcopal town blinked up at Father Reiss, embarrassed and hoping for the best. In his shoes, EV would have no mercy, would demand that they hear her confession to the end. She would regale them with her crimes, insist on being set upon a rack and flayed—and then forgiven. Wasn't that what religion was for? "Punish me! Tickle me!" she'd begged when she was a little girl.

A sudden burst of drama from the organ—the recessional. Father Reiss's nuclear family exploded from the pew with a sudden ferocious energy that reminded EV of Mei-Mei hot-waxing her eyebrows in the bathroom. She drew wax over her brow, pressed a cloth against the arch and ripped the hairs away. Zip, zip!

"Doesn't it hurt?" EV asked, impressed.

"Like hell," said Mei-Mei.

EV put away her sketchbook and pencil and followed the

others through the flung-open doors, where the congregation usually paused to shake Father Reiss's hand on the porch, though he did not appear now. She went immediately around to the parish house for the snack. She loved the careful way the altar guild made the sandwiches, the same way every time, according to an ancient recipe: They cut circles of white bread with a jam jar, spread butter on one side, then laid on damp slivers of boiled chicken, or peeled cucumbers soaked in salted water.

Old Mrs. Fiske stood at the long trestle table with a sandwich in a napkin in her hand. She was nearly blind behind her punishing black glasses; she smiled blindly at EV. "Wasn't he just great?" she said. "I think it's marvelous when a man stands up and says, 'I was wrong!' I wish we weren't losing him. Awful business. Is that EV Hellman?"

EV admitted it.

"Of course you are," said Mrs. Fiske. "Where is your beautiful mother, dear?"

"At home." Mei-Mei hardly ever went to St. Vitus on Sunday mornings; she stayed home and read Sylvia Plath or John Updike or Philip Roth in bed. But she made EV go. She said, "A soul not inoculated in compulsory religion is open to any infection."

"What about you?" EV asked.

"Already rotten to the core."

At one end of the long refreshment table, the altar guild poured coffee from a silver urn into pale blue cups and saucers. At the other end, they poured tea. The altar guild divided everyone up that way—"Coffee or tea?"—as if preferences were extremes, like *black and white* or *boys and girls*.

The choir hung their robes. Jeanne and Ruby Reiss made a silvery trace through the parish house, spoke to no one and walked out again. Father Reiss never appeared at all. Why should he absorb their compassion? What were sandwiches to him on a day like this? EV herself ate five; they were small.

She walked out back of the rectory, alongside the cemetery, and saw him bent over the stone wall, plucking dandelions from between the stones. "Father Reiss," she said, "I wanted to say good-bye."

He turned and his hand went out, an automatic gesture. His lips—and the deep declivities on either side of his nose—were chapped and raw-looking. She had only wanted, really, to touch him. She dug into her Danish school bag, pulled out the sketchbook and tore off the drawing of Jeanne and Ruby. Father Reiss looked down at the paper in his hand. "A drawing! Thank you, EV; I will enjoy it," he said.

"It's your wife and daughter."

He looked down. "Of course it is."

"I just wanted to say, you don't have to worry. I'll never tell."

His face mobilized, remained bright.

"Hold on one minute, dear."

He jogged around the rectory and returned with a ten-speed bicycle. "I'd like you to have this," he said.

"Why?" EV took the bike by the handlebars, which were curved downward, like a ram's horns. "Just kidding," she said.

Father Reiss pressed his index finger neatly into the declivity above his upper lip—the philtrum, it was called—to suggest silence and complicity, and bent slightly toward her. "It's hot," he said.

"Cool," said EV.

He watched her go, then looked down at the drawing in his hand, a competent portrait of a woman and a girl. It showed him some fact of his wife and daughter he couldn't have seen with his own eyes: the literal, even somewhat impersonal stamp of reproduction, the essentially businesslike nature of existence. It made his teeth chatter. He walked along the wall to the rectory, pulling dandelions—the irritation produced by the weed mitigated by the satisfaction of pulling it—from the interstices in the granite until he came to the heavy front door of the rector's residence, nothing so simple or natural as "his house." He did not get to have a house of his own, though he sometimes dreamed he had one, or sketched architectural ideas on the backs of his sermons in progress. Now—although nothing mattered in the airless, hollow universe—maybe he could.

He slipped the drawing into the waistband of his boxer shorts and entered the residence by the side door. He'd removed his cassock earlier, in the sacristy. Now he wore khaki slacks, a shirt and his collar.

He climbed the stairs to the room he shared with his wife. (No, Jeanne hadn't sent him away; she might not—she washed her hands more than ever, but they'd had relations several times since his disgrace.) She seemed more receptive after his betrayal, more awake, the intimacy a collusion between them. He set his watch on the bureau. He removed EV's drawing from the band of his shorts, folded it carefully and laid it between the pages of the Bible by his bed—Jeanne would never look there. (Was the drawing incriminating? Yes, it was. A drawing given to him by a young girl. It could ruin his life—but his life was already ruined.) Other incriminating pieces of paper in his Bible presented themselves: an old slip on which he had written, "First, they prayed; and then they needed God"; another slip, this one with just one line in red, like a fortune cookie: "behold, I am vile." He stripped away his clothes and dressed in shorts (Goode School Lacrosse), a T-shirt, athletic socks and sneakers. But just as he prepared to run out the door, the telephone rang. It was Goddard Byrd. "I've been thinking about you, old man. You'd better come by the house and have a drink." And so instead of running around and around the track at Goode, spending himself in concentric circles of mind-numbing effort, Bill Reiss ran to the town square, past the handsomely preserved stocks, where a man like himself might be left to rot, and then up to the red-hot front door of God's house, which he pecked at with the brass jaw of a lion. There he spent the afternoon drinking gin with the fallen head, his old ally, in his lair, talking about Nixon and the crimes of other men.

1975 and after

Why We Love Hell

One Sunday morning—it must have been during the March break—Mei-Mei drove me out to the peat bog at the edge of Cape Wilde to see the damage the beavers had done. She showed me birch tree trunks gnawed to pencil points, the meat of the tree beneath the bark pink and injured-looking. We walked along frozen dirt and dry grass, the scabbed winter surface of earth, and surveyed the pond, the dam and the domes of wadded mud and sticks—the lodges the beavers made to live in. The beavers *engineered* their lodges, Mei-Mei said; they did it mathematically, by instinct, though she didn't elaborate on that aspect, as engineering and math don't interest her. She pointed out how the entrances and exits were both underwater, for security; ramps from the entrances led to platforms where the beavers lived. It was perfectly mathematical, Mei-Mei said, and yet, someone, somewhere, had made a fatal mistake, for the house filled up with water. Even though beavers can hold their breath for up to fifteen minutes, something went terribly, terribly wrong, and all the beaver family drowned.

This is the kind of story that grabs Mei-Mei, a story of miscalculation, accident, death—especially death by drowning—and explains the world to her. This is Mei-Mei's sermon: "Why We Love Hell." Any sketch of her would be incomplete without the list of bad ends she pours out to me on Sunday mornings when, instead of more formal moral cleansing, we now spill parables via telephone. The man who lost his private parts to an explosion on a gas toilet. The man who had a sex change at midlife. (Can you imagine, asks Mei-Mei, waking up as a middle-aged woman?) The disgruntled man who killed his estranged wife with a two-by-four and encased her in fiberglass. The woman with three children who murdered a Wellesley math professor (emerita) with a stone cat over a money dispute; a former classmate of mine who hanged herself with a bedsheet in the county jail. I could go on; I will go on. The murderer who came into Smith's house; Smith offered the murderer a beer, which the murderer drank, and then he went on down the road and murdered someone else. The man whose wife tried for twenty years to commit suicide every time he left her alone. The former chair of the historical society whose wife developed Alzheimer's. He went out to a meeting but forgot his key. When he returned to the house, she wouldn't open the door because she didn't remember who he was; he lost three fingers to frostbite, rapping on the door all night. The moral of Mei-Mei's stories is always the same. Disaster is a genius, lurking. Be careful! Don't die!

Mei-Mei's identity is wrapped in her tragedy. She is defined, engrossed and fulfilled by it. Maybe for this reason, I am a relentless optimist. As a small child, I learned to see in the dark. My pupils grew until they found the bright spot in a black hole. Optimism boils constantly in me, like one of those endless Sunday stews on the back burner—the tough cut of my soul, relentlessly tenderizing over a flame. To her, the grimmest stories make sense.

1980 and after

A Cold Case

1.

. . . we see the rare virtue of a strong individual vitality, and the rare virtue of thick walls, and the rare virtue of interior spaciousness. Oh, man! admire and model thyself after the whale! Do thou, too, remain warm among ice. Do thou, too, live in this world without being of it.

—HERMAN MELVILLE, *Moby-Dick*

The story could begin anywhere, anytime, say the end of the 1970s, say Northampton, Massachusetts, with desire or violence. My new housemates and I made dinner for a couple of boys. We said things like "Do you think gender matters? Gender doesn't matter. What matters is if you like the person." And "Even liking the person doesn't matter. What matters is the human connection."

"Matters to what? What matters?" we asked.

"That's just it," Karim said.

We took off our clothes, a gesture that Karim, an interdisciplinary studies major and slightly older than the rest of us, called "consensual sensuality." We spent the night on the couches in the living room, engaged in delicate and subtle politics, and in the morning were casual and cruel over coffee.

"What are you doing for winter break?" someone asked.

Plans bloomed like showy annuals: internships with the Shakespeare Company or the Women's Health Collective; meetings of the Clamshell Alliance; sit-ins for divestiture in South Africa.

"Nothing is going to happen to any of you, ever," Karim said. He himself was about to go to the Amazon. He had just come back from India, where he'd lived in an ashram, studied yoga, bathed lepers. He described the method he'd used for not getting run over by buses or cars: a technique of walking with exquisite slowness directly into traffic. But then he said that in India pedestrians had no rights; a pedestrian who was hit by a truck was expected to apologize. (Karim himself possessed an aggressive, righteous humility.) His contempt for English literature and Western civilization was complete.

"What do these books teach you, that privileged white people from the West are the center of the universe, the names of flowers in Kew Gardens, how to flense a leviathan?" He plucked my copy of *Moby-Dick,* which I hadn't cracked yet, from the coffee table. "The interior thoughts of dead white men," Karim said—the first time I'd heard anyone speak with such direct contempt for white men who were dead.

"The real question," Karim said, hefting and then tossing the book down among the bikini panties and bottles of Mateus, "the *only* question, is, What will you do in life to offset what you do to drain the planet's resources by breathing, eating, living in a house, driving a car, probably producing another child or two for the earth to feed? I have lived in a cardboard box in Egypt, okay? I have bathed lepers in Calcutta. Okay? What has all this freedom, paid for in napalm, taught you about the world? What have you experienced, really, really? What will you do to mitigate the impact of your life?" He reached down and massaged his penis, amusing himself while he waited to be surprised. But I could think of nothing—not yet.

2.

Much of a man's character will be found betokened
in his backbone. I would rather feel your spine
than your skull, whoever you are.
—HERMAN MELVILLE, *Moby-Dick*

Junior year, my roommate, Jess, borrowed my little black dress to go out on a date. We were the same size and shape—though I'd already begun my secret practice of self-denial—and we had the same qualities of character, sincerity and earnestness, which I already despised. As she poked pearls into her ears, Jess said, "I'm not going to sleep with this guy. I'm not going to sleep with anyone until I'm married."

"Why not?" I asked her. "For what possible reason?"

Jess removed a blow-dryer from the top drawer of her dresser. "I want to keep my place in heaven," she said.

"You're kidding."

"No, I'm not," Jess said. "There's a place in heaven for every Catholic unless they, you know, screw up."

"What about the rest of us?"

"You'll go to hell," Jess said matter-of-factly. She bent at the waist, turned her hair upside down and blew it out. When she finished, she rewound the cord around the blow-dryer and put it back in her drawer.

Jess started out premed, but it was too hard. She almost flunked out her first year, taking biology, chemistry and calculus. She went to the library at all hours, but it made me sad whenever I saw Jess's tidy pages of notes. That wasn't how serious work was done, I felt—with diligence, neatness and care. Jess spent most of her time at the library, trying to keep her grades up so she could make the most of her life and not end up spending it putting the green bulb into stoplights, like her mother did in the old factory. For fun, she led the a cappella group, as she'd done in high school. The medley she sang at the opening of every concert pricked my own convoluted desire for jazz and sex, and I used to sing it word for word—my own version of her voice yawping out lyrics from *Showboat* in the shower—until I discovered that everyone in the dorm could hear.

Premed was an ambition for Jess, not a gift or a passion, and finally, fearing for her full scholarship, she switched to English literature. "Because it's easy," she said.

"It's not that easy," I said.

Jess rolled her eyes. "Believe me, it's easy. I already know how to read." She didn't have much patience for literature, though. She found Henry James "boring," D. H. Lawrence "pornographic," Virginia Woolf "wordy." She liked James Joyce—but only *Dubliners*. She preferred story and action; she'd been the editor of her high school newspaper. She loved meeting people, shaping news, and changed to journalism.

We drifted apart. Apart from superficial differences—I was greedy and unsupervised, Jess devout and Catholic—she reminded me too much of myself: cheerful, literal, soft, pliant. I don't know what I reminded her of, but in November, Jess applied to change roommates. I didn't object, but by Thanksgiving neither of us had made other arrangements.

"It's not that big a deal," I said. "December, January. Then February, March, April and May. I can stand it. Can you?"

During winter break, we had no classes, were urged to find meaningful work exploring careers, advancing social justice or reveling in the arts. Jess found an internship at a radio station outside Denver. She'd worked in the dining room all fall to pay for her flight. She'd live with an aunt and uncle in a nearby suburb, just a bus ride away. Her conservative parents approved;

she'd be safe. She even bought herself a cheap wedding ring to keep herself honest.

My great-aunt Ruth died around Thanksgiving and left me a surprise legacy, a matter of a few hundred dollars, which, she stipulated in her will, must be spent on "self-improvement." Aunt Ruth had famously been "wild" until sometime before I was born, and her father, my great-grandfather, brought in a doctor to scramble her frontal lobe. After the operation, nothing new ever happened to Aunt Ruth. She worked at the pharmacy soda fountain for thirty-five years, had no friends, no lovers or husbands. No one ever asked her what she thought or felt, or what had happened to her; everyone knew what had happened. (She'd been "wild.") After Aunt Ruth died (ruptured appendix, staph infection), Mei-Mei got a telephone call and we had to run down to the boardinghouse where Aunt Ruth had lived and remove an outrageous mass of pornographic magazines from under her bed. She was the princess and the pea of pornography, her mattress all in lumps.

Mei-Mei, kneeling, dropped the men's magazines into a Seagram's box. "Don't you see what this means?" she asked. "The procedure freed Aunt Ruth of her anxiety, but not of her yearning."

"Where did she buy them? How? When?" I asked, impressed.

"Oh, she was clever," Mei-Mei said. "Plus, she worked at the pharmacy."

The magazines filled the Seagram's box. "We can't just throw these out," Mei-Mei said. "Where would we throw them?" She decided to keep the magazines under her own bed. In the early part of winter break, while Mei-Mei worked, I read them all. Aunt Ruth's magazines were my first real experience of multiple points of view, in which I played the reader, the watcher, the consumer, the pleasure seeker, yet also indentified with the object, the woman, a voluptuous form of myself, my gender archetype. I became the watcher and the watched, the subject and the object. My critical awareness developed, too—I became critical of the pictures, looked for ways in which they assumed maleness in the viewer, and yet also spoke to my own desires to be seen, to see myself. I learned the structure, the shape of the sexual story. The magazines called to me more strongly than *Moby-Dick,* which I'd been assigned for a course called Leviathans of Literature: Scaling the Immense American Novel.

What did Aunt Ruth expect me to do with her money? Make up for her lost life? Should I read her gift as an expansive, bold gesture, or a pathetic, desperate one? The sum was too small to dent tuition or loans, so I spent it all on airfare and a hotel on an island in the Caribbean during winter break—the same island where the Rebozos family once had a house, and where Carole Faust was born. I didn't tell anyone except Jess, out of some perverse desire, probably, to shock her. (I told Mei-Mei a temporary job in the registrar's office had opened up; I'd always been secretive, like Ruth.) At school, I packed a straw bag, then took a taxi to the airport; I'd never gone anywhere on my own before.

That was the first year of CNN—news all the time. Ronald Reagan campaigned for president; a volcano erupted in Washington State; America boycotted the Olympic games in Moscow to protest the Soviet invasion of Afghanistan; Mark David Chapman murdered John Lennon. News spooled out all year, twenty-four hours of every day. I paid little attention; in fact, the constant stream of news drove me deep into *Moby-Dick,* which turned out to contain some fairly urgent dispatches.

3.

The intense concentration of self in the middle of such a heartless immensity, my God! Who can tell it? Mark, how

when sailors in a dead calm bathe in the
open ocean—mark how closely they hug their ship
and only coast along her sides.
—HERMAN MELVILLE, *Moby-Dick*

I took a taxi down a boulevard of dying palm trees and checked into the Hotel Pamplemousse—"the most economical lodging on the island," according to the brochure. Lizards clung to the stucco walls and occasionally leapt upon cockroaches, which stood like islands in the linoleum sea. Young women swam in the pool all day, or chatted with men, and I realized from their qualities of earnestness and cheerfulness that they were probably prostitutes. While I unpacked, the bellman unlocked and opened the door to the room without knocking. He walked in, farther in than necessary, and held out a thin towel. Unnerved, I sat down at the desk and wrote a postcard to Jess: "The Hotel Pamplemousse is a hellhole. It's the sort of place where the bellman walks into your room unannounced and without knocking and offers you a towel, then leers into your suitcase. Hope you have better luck in Denver." Denver . . . it occurred to me that I did not have Jess's address in Denver. She hadn't given it to me; I hadn't asked.

I left the postcard on the desk and went out, past the lizards on the stucco walls, down some dank steps and into the town, where I walked up and down along the quay. I walked until dusk through a neighborhood of brightly painted bungalows with rotting front steps, losing and then finding my way. Finally I turned into an alley that looked as if it might be a shortcut back to the hotel.

A boy—a man in the provisional way that I was a woman—immediately seized me by the arm. There were other boys in the alley, each of whom looked about twelve years old. They all wore brightly colored print shorts and no shirts. "This is a bad street," the boy-man whispered confidentially in accented English, as if he knew all about the possibilities of the humid little city. "The knives," he said, "are in the pants!"

He walked with me down the alley, past the boys, who whispered suggestively, and into the main street. I'd been right about the shortcut: The Hotel Pamplemousse stood serenely on the corner. We sat in the lobby. He told me his name was Fabio; he came originally from Italy, where he'd been crushed by lack of opportunity. He talked urgently for an hour about the dangers of the island, the sights and his qualifications as a guide: "I am no smoker, no drinker. I employ my time." He told me about a boat I must take to the island across the bay—the best beaches, the best swimming. "You walk down the beach as far as you like. Nobody there," he said. "You are solo, alone." We sat together demurely in the lobby; then Fabio insisted on taking me out to dinner. "It is necessary that you permit me the pleasure," he said.

We went to a place called La Chatte, where we drank strong rum drinks and ate steaks. It was the best restaurant I had ever been to—white tablecloths, cloth napkins. In one corner of the dining room, near the bar, a dance floor glowed under the glittering facets of a disco light. A beautiful woman, Chinese, dressed all in red, wearing a black eye patch over one eye, danced there alone.

Fabio told me different, slightly conflicting stories about himself: He'd lived on the island for a year; he traveled often; he studied business in Italy and lived with his mother amid the magnificent artistic patrimony of Perugia. His white shirt glowed blue in the light; he smelled of cologne. He ordered for both of us and commanded me in his beautiful accented English to eat and drink. "You must feed *your body,*" he said, as if my body were a hungry animal. Some people expressed themselves sensually, I realized. They tasted their food, enjoyed their bodies, liked being looked at. As we walked out of the restaurant after dinner, Fabio pointed to the woman wearing the eye patch. "Watch out for her," he said.

"Why?"

"She is sometimes my lover."

We walked through the warm, dirty streets back to my hotel. Fabio took my arm, a gesture I didn't expect, and walked me up the steps of the Pamplemousse. Inside, he steered me into the seedy bar off the lobby, where we sat down on a vinyl sofa and he ordered two coffees. I'd been on the island for about five hours and felt amazed by the progress I'd made.

"What do you do here?" I asked him.

"How do I say? I am sometimes a gigolo," he said. He took my hand when he said it, his face very serious. "You understand?"

"You mean women pay you to make love to them," I said.

"Sometimes, yes," he said, "it's true."

"Well, I'm not going to pay you to make love to me," I said.

"Not necessary," he agreed.

Ordinary conversation was impossible between us. That helped. He wore his body like beautiful clothing made just for him. He covered me with it, then pulled back so we both could see. It was the first time I felt part of a human transaction, sexually, and not as if I'd simply given over the insistently desired thing. He put one hand between my legs and said, "Show me her." And I did. A dense, surprising pleasure ran like current between us. Communication improved. Against the silence of the room I listened to the sounds we made—wet, generative sounds, as if we were actually melting into each other. I realized what this was: I invited Fabio to enter me, and he entered the vast, indefinite interior. For a little while the terrible lonely immensity of my body was colonized, filled with Fabio's uncircumcised and lively penis and something else, my heart fluttering in the dark space like a cornered butterfly. I envisioned my individual life as a dark belly from whose depths I might occasionally reach a hand to another person. My body spoke to Fabio with thrilling directness. His fingers entered my mouth and ear, and moved communicatively.

In the morning, my new lover was gone. I put on my bathing suit and dropped a towel, suntan oil and *Moby-Dick* into my straw bag. While I brushed my teeth, I found a watch on a shelf above the sink, a heavy, expensive-looking lattice of gold and platinum. It chilled me to find a piece of Fabio left behind, and I left the watch where I'd found it. On the ferry, I wondered, What if the bellman steals the watch? What if Fabio blames me? On the island, a long allée of palm trees led to a loud knot of sunbathers on the beach. As Fabio had suggested, I walked until the bathers were no longer in the picture and laid my towel on the sand.

I opened up *Moby-Dick* and read "not clamorous for pardon, but grateful for punishment." The line's delicate resonance induced a pang of complicated pleasure and opened up new vistas in my mind, from which I was immediately distracted by Fabio standing above me, serious in the sun.

He peeled away his jeans to reveal a European bikini. A waiter from the cabana walked the quarter mile down the beach with an empty tray on his palm and offered cocktails. Fabio said no, the beach was not to drink, and the waiter retreated.

"You will have lines on your body if you wear a bathing suit," Fabio advised. *Your body*. He removed a watch from his wrist and laid it on my straw bag.

"Is that your watch?" I asked him. "You left it in my room."

"No problem," he said. "I go there."

"How did you get in?"

"The bellman is kind and allows me to enter," he said, and untied my top.

In the afternoon, we walked back to the boat together. Fabio said he had a *faccenda;* he would come to the hotel later. I took myself out to dinner at one of the overpriced cafés along the promenade and read *Moby-Dick* until the words grew too dim to see.

Hours later, the door to my room opened suddenly—a bright window in the dark. I thought it must be Jess just back from her carrel at the library. But Jess turned into the bellman standing in the door. I jumped up and ran at him violently with my fists. "Get out! Get out!" The door closed in my face. "Sorry, sorry—wrong room," the bellman said, and left me pounding at my own door.

Thereafter, I slept less.

I spent the next day at the same spot on the beach, reading *Moby-Dick* in the sun and vaguely expecting Fabio. The man from the bar walked the quarter mile across the sand with a tray balanced on his palm and asked if I'd like a drink. Out of compassion, I ordered a rum and tonic. (He walked back across the sand, then returned again with the drink, then walked back across the sand to the bar again. Still later, he returned, inquired about my well-being and took the glass away.) I went for a swim. Later, while I ate a conch burger at the bar, the stool next to mine toppled over with a great noise. I'd been too engrossed in my book to see what happened—maybe I had kicked it. I recognized the Chinese woman with the eye patch walking calmly away from me toward the ocean. She wore a red bikini and a rope of pearls around her waist and enormous sunglasses and tall espadrilles. I picked up my napkin and saw that someone had scratched the words *FUCK US* into the wood of the bar with a knife.

At the hotel, I found Fabio sitting at my desk, looking out the window at the swimming pool.

"What are you doing here?" I asked.

"I came to make love to you," he said.

"You take your work too seriously," I said. "You're too used to being needed." I sat down on the bed and took off my sandals.

He stood up and held out a small box wrapped in paper. "For you."

I didn't reach for the box—for some impersonal, irrelevant gift.

"You are married in the U.S.?" he said.

"Of course not."

"So why do you come to the island, to meet new people?" He ran one finger slowly down my face and put the box in my hand. It wasn't really wrapped; all I had to do was lift the lid. Chocolates.

"*Baci,*" he said. "Sweet kisses to remember me."

"Thank you," I said, repelled by all these ideas—chocolate, sweet kisses, Fabio as a memory.

He put his cool hands around my sunburned back. "I don't want that you forget your boyfriend," he said. "I want only to feel hot with you."

Next day the same: Fabio gone when I woke. I took the boat to the island again, walked through the allée of palms and spent the day reading *Moby-Dick* in the sand. I returned to my room around four o'clock and found Fabio sitting in the window, watching the women swim in the pool. He had a kitten in his lap, scruffy and black, wild and terrified—he must have picked it up in the street on his way. "I have you a gift," he said.

"Are you crazy?" I said. "What am I going to do with a cat? I'm leaving in two days."

He made a gesture with his hands that demonstrated the infinite possibilities of a kitten. "*La chatte* keeps you company when you are here, and then you can take it home on the airplane," he said.

"I can't take *la chatte* on the plane."

He shrugged. "When you go, you put it on your little balcony and tell it to find a new house."

We sat on the bed in our underwear, the kitten purring between us. "I cannot stay with you tonight," Fabio said. "The Chinese lady feel jealous. This because she have buy me a car, a nice Trans Am."

La chatte's legs and paws stiffened and trembled as it dreamed. Fabio swept it from the sheets with the back of his hand and the creature meowed and ran under the bed. I reached out for him from the dark well; I could almost see my hand rising up from that darkness, groping its way toward Fabio's skin.

We spent the next day sunbathing. He watched while I read *Moby-Dick*. Fabio never read anything; he was a master of repose. Late in the afternoon, he said, "You became red as a langoustine." It was true. That night, he stayed in the room and ran ice down my back. The ice felt cold, but Fabio's body radiated a kind of insistent heat.

When I woke again, dawn had turned the sheets an eerie blue. The kitten mewed from under the bed.

I may have been delirious, sunstruck. Fabio and the Chinese woman seemed to be in my room, the Chinese woman doing exactly the things with Fabio that I had done, and Fabio repeating every gesture: his hand around her hair, his fingers in her mouth. Up close, she and Fabio were not as glamorous as I'd first seen them; they had missing teeth and holes in their heads, skin scraped off, scabs. I realized I had lost my ring of keys, so I climbed into the rickety elevator, which no longer operated smoothly on its pulley, but lurched down. When I went outside the seedy lobby, I saw my keys glowing on the dirty ground before me, a miracle.

It was only a heat delusion. I found my own keys—a different set from the keys in the dream—safe in my straw bag. I put on my warmest, loosest clothes and kept turning pages of *Moby-Dick*. When Fabio let himself in, I got up from the bed and stumbled into him. He sat me back down and began to pull my sweater over my shoulders.

"Ow, ow!" I said.

"But it must come off," he said reasonably.

He removed my clothes as gently as he could. He unbuttoned his shirt, knelt at the bottom of the bed and pulled my cotton pants down around my ankles.

"Don't touch me," I whispered. "Everything hurts."

"It is not necessary to touch you," he said. "Only a little," touching.

The door to the room opened and the bellman stood there. I lunged at him and attacked his face with my hands until he ran away. Then I realized that I hadn't moved. I was still in the bed, alone, naked under the white sheets, the blanket a tangle at my feet. The bellman entered the room, approached the bed, then went out again. He left, on the nightstand, a half grapefruit with a maraschino cherry in the center, and a serrated spoon.

Fabio didn't come back. My skin peeled off. The kitten ran away—it flew from under the bed—the instant the bellman opened the door. I took a taxi to the airport. On the boulevard of the dying palms, the driver stopped at a traffic light and I saw a red Trans Am, driven by the one-eyed Chinese woman. In the passenger seat sat Fabio. Both of them were staring straight ahead, together in the heightened consciousness of people who enjoy being looked at.

As I returned to school, something strange happened: Jess was all over CNN. She was the headline news, wearing a turtleneck and a little woolen beanie, perfectly herself, round-cheeked and freckled, except that she had died. Not only had Jess died; she had been murdered in Colorado. Not only had she been murdered in Colorado; she had been raped, her body left on a frozen field, tortured and dead. Not only had she been raped, tortured and murdered; she had been impugned as an example of the cost of sexual freedom, a relatively new idea, an example of the result: Young women who didn't understand limits or men, putting themselves out into the world, taking buses at night. Jess's slacks—the CNN word, *slacks*—had not been recovered. She had been tied with the straps from her messenger bag and stabbed nine times in the back, apparently while performing oral sex on her murderer. The network displayed her parents as evidence, their mouths black holes of wonder. What had happened? The new news—CNN—tried to point to a moral, or a trend, or a metaphor, or a social disease. This was the beginning of something new—a way of making sudden, terrible, inexplicable events last all day, so that rings of possible meaning could be created around them. But the question of what happened to Jess was never resolved. Even now, twenty-six years later, the case is still cold.

1982

EV in New York

After college (BA, Smith College, gender studies, skin of her teeth, no distinction), EV moved to New York and found a job in retail. The store off Fifth where she worked paid the minimum; she couldn't live or eat normally. But the job had compensations: The Beautiful Living booth shimmered with bright toys, and the Show of Shoes—a smoky-mirrored aisle of pumps, stiletto heels, slingbacks, sandals, ballerinas, t-straps and thigh boots arrayed under a hot pink satin banner, BETTER THAN SEX: THE NEW CHARLIE JOURDANS—distracted her from less material yearnings. She lived in a studio sublet downtown, where she could choose between coffee or a corn muffin in the morning, a tuna-salad sandwich or a bottle of wine at night. She blew out the pilot light on her old Royal Rose range—she didn't need a stove—and never went to the movies or bought a newspaper. Six midmornings a week, she roused her adrenaline by leaving for work twenty minutes late to lurch uptown on the local. Then she ran manically down Fifty-seventh Street, rushed under the awning and through familiar stalls of shoes and boots trimmed in Carpet Python, Baltic Leopard and Brook Mink. (Even here, at the center of the universe, everything worth having came from somewhere else.) She endangered Italian pottery and glassware on her way to the Fabulous Food booth, where she worked until six, bagging expensive candy in cellophane.

One day, she noticed a pair of red suede pumps lined with a black material so shiny that it looked wet, and she felt, just beneath her heart, the chemical dilation of drugs or love. Even with her discount, the shoes cost more than EV earned in two weeks, but she was allowed to put them on her account and take them home. For a few days, she kept them in a formal still life on the table where she ate. The shoes were too perfect and new to sully in the street; to wear them once into the store to work would ruin them forever. But then her neighbor down the hall—ancient, scary Juliet from 4C—stopped by with a tub of supermarket potato salad and ruined them anyway. "You put shoes on a table!" Juliet told her. "You just gave yourself a whole life of bad luck!"

EV seized the shoes by the heels and let them hang off her fingers. But EV's fate was nothing to Juliet, who leaned against the rotting doorjamb and unfurled complaints about her favorite enemy, an old wreck named McCarthy, who lived across the hall.

"He pished on the floor in the bathroom!" Juliet told EV. "I cleaned it up!"

"That was rude," EV agreed. She looked around for another place to keep the shoes off the floor, but the table and her futon were the only furniture. She laid the shoes on her futon, where they immediately appeared so horribly ordinary that she picked them up again and put them on. The smooth lining resisted her gritty toes, but the opening—the vamp—felt sensual, sucky. EV listened to Juliet's deluded, improbable stories: McCarthy's violent history, the landlord's theft of a check from her mailbox, the conspiracy among the United States, Germany and the People's Republic of China to finish off the Jews by dosing Chinese and kosher food with the poison MSG.

When Juliet left, EV locked the door with the dead bolt and walked back and forth across her apartment. The telephone rang: her neighbor from downstairs, P. Cornblum, calling to complain. "Little Angel Feet," he said, "I need quiet for my work. Please take off your shoes when you tramp!"

EV didn't argue. She admired P. Cornblum for understanding and asserting his needs—for silence, as an example. Also, he was aristocratic; he had his clothes dry-cleaned. She removed the shoes and saw that the perfect black lining was dulled already from contact with her feet. She'd ruined them already.

The serious, deranging conflict in the building didn't center on EV; it swirled around her. How would Juliet from 4C kill McCarthy in 4B and when? Suspense ran like a wire between their two front doors. McCarthy roared threats from his rooms, and Juliet performed witchy, symbolic gestures. Only EV in 4A stood between them.

McCarthy and Juliet had lived in their apartments forever. McCarthy got a monthly VA check in the mail; Juliet lived on cat tuna, potato salad and tripe. Legends of their low rent varied—twenty-five dollars, seventy dollars a month. Whatever it was, it kept both of them climbing the steep, greasy stairs and sharing their WC, a formidable sump in the middle of the hallway that provided the main provocation and bond between them. The landlord had long ago given up making repairs on either of their places. The door to the WC sometimes stuck open on the peeling linoleum, and EV could see, as she hurried past on her way to work, the terrible lip of the toilet, the pocked mirror above the tiny, filthy sink. P. Cornblum was more pointed. The whole fourth floor ought to be condemned, he told the landlord. It stank like a pisshole in France.

Sometimes, EV felt an urge to slide them on and walk around her living room with a glass of wine in her hand. The sound of her shoes on the floor made her feel alive.

One such evening, P. Cornblum called and invited EV downstairs. She went immediately, clattering across the linoleum, and rang the bell. He opened the door and let her in. Then he turned the beam of his attention toward the ceiling and the radiator pipes. "Every sound you make comes through here," he told her.

EV looked up at the barrier through which P. Cornblum experienced the shuddering force of her personality. But the ceiling was blank and white, and the pipes, wrapped like old athletic injuries in gauzy yellow asbestos, were quiet and dead.

He'd stuck yellow squares of paper all over his walls. Each square had a word or a few words, or else a crude sketch drawn on it. "CHURCH BELLS," "LIGHTNING CAUSED BY ELECTRICITY," "SYSTEMS THEORY"; a lightning bolt, an eagle—or some kind of bird.

EV touched one.

"These are Post-it notes," he said. "One of the major innovations of the decade." He bent over a pad of the notes, wrote "3M Corporation," peeled away the note and stuck it on her chest. "There," he said. "Go buy yourself some stock. Then you'll make a killing and move uptown and I can get some work done."

Sometimes at the mailboxes in the foyer, he was intimate and critical with her, as if there might already be a personal relationship between them. "You don't even look at the *Times,*" he told her once. "How do you expect anything to happen to you? You're not serious."

"How do you know I'm not serious?" she asked him.

"You should get a library card, look up Susan Sontag," he told her, snapping his mailbox shut. "Everything is a metaphor."

EV wrote it down quickly on her hand with a pen once he was out of sight—"Serious, Sontag, metaphor."

As usual, she left for work at the last possible moment. She drank her coffee near the window, propped her feet in her red suede shoes on the sill and watched the Italian women across the street lean out of their windows. Then she left everything as it was, her shoes on the sill, the radio on. She slid her feet into the flat ballet slippers she wore to work, pushed the heavy front door open and dug in her coat pocket for the key.

"Oh, hi!" she said in surprise, because Juliet was standing very close, at McCarthy's door opposite, holding a claw hammer in one hand and a raw supermarket chicken in the other. A thin rope of white hair hung down her back. Juliet didn't answer EV, but raised the chicken up against the door and tried to drive a nail through some skin with her hammer. McCarthy's door rattled and the blows shook the hall. EV slammed her own door to close it, but the doorjamb failed; a slice of wood spongy with old nail holes dropped to the floor. Unlike McCarthy's wooden door, which dated from a more trusting era, EV's was heavy and metal, gouged with two Medecos and a police lock. The frame had rotted, though. The door leaned forward slowly, forcing Juliet and then EV aside. Then it burst its remaining hinges and jammed up against McCarthy's door like a barricade. EV's efforts to pry her door loose only made the situation worse. From behind his door came McCarthy's thin, hysterical voice. "No you don't!" he shouted. "You're not taking my door! I'll kill you first!"

"We're not taking your door. Worse! Worse!" cried Juliet. She shot EV an incriminating, conspiratorial look, then walked back down the hall with the hammer and the chicken hanging down together from the blue lace of veins that was her hand.

"Hold on, Mr. McCarthy; I'll go get help," EV said, but no voice came from behind the door, just a hopeless banging, a pathetic twisting of the knob.

She ran downstairs and knocked at the door of 3A. She knew P. Cornblum would be at home. He lived and worked at home, in a bubble of silence, ripe for disruption. He appeared at the door with a finger on one temple, as if holding something in. Behind him, the Post-it notes were gone. Rows of books in wooden shelves held up the sources that validated his opinions. P. Cornblum was pasty from his indoor life. A set of earphones hung from his neck, hooked up to nothing. He had beautiful, soft, full lips, chilly, myopic eyes and black-framed glasses. He disliked EV in an almost impersonal way that she respected. Often, at night, she dreamed of him.

"Banging away early today," he said.

"I was on my way to work," EV told him. "My front door came off—fell over. It's stuck up against McCarthy's front door."

"What do you mean, 'stuck up against'?"

EV tried to describe the imperfect phrase with her hands. "He can't get out. The door fell off and now it's stuck. *I'm* stuck."

He wore a pair of indoor-outdoor slippers, rubber-soled and shearling-lined. He climbed the flight of stairs to EV's floor and, waving EV away as if she were an insect, prized the door free. "I won't ask how you managed to achieve this," he said.

EV smiled and hung her head in shame.

Her apartment stood agape. Instead of going to work, she had to call the super, who lived in a building a few blocks away. It wasn't the first time she had broken something unbreakable. At her job, EV routinely did damage to liqueur-filled bonbons and fancy boxed lunches. She'd also broken the pneumatic tube the store used for all its money transactions, blocking the urgent traffic of money and receipts. In seventy-five years of business, this had never happened before. Her boss, the candy buyer, blamed EV, and actually stopped speaking to her. This led to some confusion about the size of the bags EV was supposed to use for packing a new breed of chocolate dog, and she had to spend hours repacking them all.

"Are you for real?" the candy buyer asked EV. For some reason, the remark stung.

"And don't write stuff on your hand with a pen," the candy buyer added. "It looks trashy."

All the salespeople at the store had a Look—hair short and moppy, or long and pulled back severely; black-black or bleached white. The candy buyer was pale and stick-thin, with short, vigorously ratted, very black hair. She was a vegetarian and ate nothing but candy all day, standing up and pacing around the Fabulous Food booth like a nervous animal.

As a new hire, EV was entitled to a haircut in the store's salon. "Go ahead," the candy buyer urged her, "Do some damage."

The haircut came free, a benefit instead of Blue Cross. So EV booked an appointment at the salon and put herself in the hands of a Dr. Johnson, who refused to cut EV's hair until his associate had put color in it. A child-size woman who spoke a rapid-fire Slavic language appeared with a muddy blue substance in a ceramic bowl. "I don't want blue hair!" EV protested, but the woman merely shrugged, as if EV had spoken some arbitrary words about the weather. The dyeing and cutting took three or four hours. EV sat in a chair in front of a mirror while Dr. Johnson shaved off part of her hair with a razor. He chatted philosophically while he worked: "Sometimes I see a boy who looks cute and then I realize that the boy is a girl dressed like a boy, walking like a boy, with the attitude of a boy and yet is a girl, slight and not too hairy, and I think how happy this would make my mother if she knew."

Her hair turned out not blue, as EV had feared, but bright pink. "Is better," the colorist assured EV. "Is radical."

The haircut—wild and rather flattering, EV thought—was free, but the color cost big money, a list of charges on a tag that

Dr. Johnson waved in front of her face. EV apologized; she had four dollars in her wallet. Dr. Johnson left her, to call the police, EV assumed. Instead, he arranged to have the bill and a tip put on EV's account.

She took the elevator downstairs. The candy buyer said, "You took too long and you look like hell. I should fire you right now."

Instead, she sent EV up to the windowless storeroom on twelve, where the air was gritty with sugar. EV sat on the floor and filled a hundred bags with dogs. She thought of Karim Brazir, living in his box in Egypt or bathing lepers in India—she could be like that. Or she could simply be a hunger artist, a self-denier, and discipline herself that way.

She tied bows around the tops of the bags and carried them all downstairs in a metal handbasket. The candy buyer lifted one of the bags from the basket and let it drop. "These bows are shit," she said.

EV looked at the bags already nestled into their expensive display and saw that it was true. The candy buyer's loops were tied shiny-side up, her bows expert. EV's looked as if a child had tied them. The candy buyer reached behind her and unfurled a piece of ribbon from a winch on the wall. Her fingers worked at manic speed, doing four or five things at once, twisting the bag, looping the ribbon around the neck and tying a bow roughly—but perfectly—so that the whole package was unified and all the chocolate dog muzzles faced front. "Like *that,*" the buyer said. "One step. Can you do it?" Her eyes had a crashed, glassy look.

"So you make the bow *while* you twist the bag," EV said, trying to sound teachable. Maybe she could be a teacher.

"Can you do it?"

EV took up the ribbon. "I think I can," she said.

While EV worried about the time and her job, the super nailed the old frame back into the wall and rehung EV's door. McCarthy, liberated finally, emerged from his prison wearing gray undershorts and an undershirt, and lurched down the hall into the WC. EV locked up, then rode the subway uptown, although she had a vivid premonition she'd be too late, that the incident with the broken door would be the last straw, something unforgivable, and it was.

"My front door came off," EV told the candy buyer when she rushed up to the booth, wheezing out the string of words she needed to explain herself. "I had to stay until the super came to rehang it. It's this heavy metal door, and it wasn't the door so much as the wall, the wooden piece attached to the wall with the nails and the hinges in it? That part was all rotten, and he had to make a new one. But in the meantime, my door was wide open, and I couldn't leave."

The candy buyer didn't even look up. "I fired you two hours ago," she said. "You're history. I went to have them get your check ready, but it turns out you owe the store. So my advice is, clear out fast and don't come back. I'll tell them you moved back to New England or whatever." This small kindness was too much. EV was seized by fury. She backed into the Beautiful Living booth, shaking loose a Provençal plate, which shattered on the floor.

A pair of hairless male hands, the hands of an assassin, reached out from the Beautiful Living booth. EV turned and ran.

She ran out the front doors of the store, down Fifty-seventh Street, then down Sixth Avenue. The city seemed fresh and brilliant; her feet, in ballet slippers, rose lightly from the hard pavement. She ran over forty blocks, until a sole tore open on a steam grate, and the suede pad flapped like a tongue. This slowed her down as she approached the branch library, which stood imposingly at the fork of two streets—the famous Gothic tower of the former women's prison. A voice called to her: "Hey, pink-haired girl."

She stopped, looked around and saw a guy about her own age—a large man, excruciatingly handsome—on the library steps. "You okay?" he asked her.

"Yes," said EV.

"Oh, because you look like you've had a terrible shock."

She smiled at him and started walking.

"I like your pink hair," he said, and then, more loudly, added, "Wait a minute. Have a little faith in human nature."

EV turned. "I have a little faith in human nature," she said.

The stranger descended to the sidewalk. "Give me your phone number, then. We could do something."

She dug into her pockets, found a pen and a yellow square of paper and wrote her name and telephone number.

He turned the paper over in his hands, read both sides. " 'Serious, Sontag.' I like it."

"Thanks," she said, and hurried back to her apartment to wait.

A raw chicken hung from the cross of wood that joined the four panels of McCarthy's front door. EV touched the breast—or was that the back? Whatever it was felt warm and poisonous. She tapped his door with the sawed-off teeth of her key. She thought he should know.

But McCarthy wouldn't answer. It wasn't unusual for him to hole up for a day or two, drinking or drunk, 'pishing,' Juliet had told her, in his kitchen sink.

For two days, EV stayed in. She tapped out small communications with the heels of her shoes, but for once P. Cornblum didn't call to complain. On the third day, she heard a rustling of plastic in the hall and went to the peephole to look. It was he—Cornblum—his face pasty and grim, his hands covered up in yellow rubber gloves. EV watched through the peephole while he pulled the soft body from the nail and dropped it into a black trash bag. She felt McCarthy's and Juliet's eyes watching through their peepholes, three eyes examining the downstairs neighbor through the deforming lenses in their unreliable doors. At least she hoped Juliet would see that it was P. Cornblum undoing her work, and not suspect EV herself.

When he'd gone, EV pulled her pink bathrobe more tightly around herself and opened the front door. McCarthy stood in the hall wearing long underwear and a yellow undershirt, his eyes red and webby with exploded capillaries. He held a saucepan in his hand as if it were a weapon. The nail in the door remained; he ran a finger over it, testing reality. "Crazy witch! She put a spell on me!" he shouted. Then he peered accusingly at EV. "Why don't you go to work?" he asked her.

"I lost my job," EV told him.

McCarthy made a noise in his throat, which might have been sympathetic, and then lurched down the hall to the WC. EV closed her door carefully. Through the metal she heard Juliet's voice ring in the hall. "Why isn't she at work? What'd she tell you?"

P. Cornblum turned Juliet in to the landlord. The episode with the chicken crossed the line.

"What line is that?" EV asked him as they crowded together in the foyer, checking their wrought-iron mailboxes. He tapped a fingernail four times against his mailbox and said, "Civility, decency, safety, sanitation."

The landlord claimed that a relative had made arrangements for the witch in 4C to go to a city home. McCarthy stood in his yellow undershirt in the doorway, clucking like a respectable citizen. "It's not right to throw her out," he told EV. "She's lived here all her life."

"We should do something," EV agreed. She clutched the drooping lobes of her pink bathrobe in one hand; the ends of her fingers felt numb.

The door to the WC swung open suddenly. "Are you kidding?" Juliet yelled down the hall. "I can't wait to get out of this stinking hellhole."

"Where will you go?" EV called back.

Juliet didn't answer, just slammed her door and clanked her police lock into place.

Then one morning, Juliet was gone. Workmen came with crowbars and hammers and tore out kitchen hardware, linoleum and plaster walls. Later, they carried in a floor-sanding machine, a pedestal sink and a toilet. McCarthy—who would never again compete for his bathroom in the hall—stood in his doorway in gray underwear, his mouth open in horror and yellow tears in his eyes.

Within a week, she'd broken her lease, packed her clothes and books. She asked McCarthy if he wanted her futon (he didn't). One night during these preparations, she had another phone call—the stranger from the library, Hans. He wanted to know if she could meet him that evening—right then, actually—at the pub down the street. He pronounced his name "Hands"—Hands Holderman. It sounded like a joke, although EV chose not to succumb to a cynical attitude. She had a little faith in human nature. The whole point of living in a difficult and dangerous city was to take risks and survive.

For the first time she wore her red shoes outside—red shoes, and a pair of jeans. Hans sat at the bar, saw her in the door and waved. She waved back. The red shoes carried her forward; her body purred like a machine. He took her hands in his and then, in a forward and romantic gesture, gave her a long, penetrating kiss. His tongue assaulted the portcullis of her teeth, and his hand on her back pulled her hair. His eyes peered insolently into hers. EV allowed it. This was experience, life. He bought her a drink, and she bought him a drink, because she did not want to be a person who simply traded something personal for something material. He didn't ask her the usual things about herself, or tell a personal story. Instead, he talked about different forms of human emotion and sexuality—affinity, attachment and limerence—the overwhelming and uncontrollable feelings of joy or despair that virtually defined the Western experience of romantic love and amounted to a compulsive avoidance of reality—versus polyamory and polyfidelity. Had she studied human sexuality at all? His own sexual makeup was that he needed a harem around him, a collection of women. Someday he would have a party and they would all meet one another, and they would not resent him at all. They would be grateful; they would see.

"What would they see?" she asked.

"What I've seen," he said. "The way I've sorted and culled and discerned. They would see the essence of themselves. You know what's the most erotic thing? Talking. I love to hear women talk. Tell me anything. Tell me your perceptions. Tell me how you think. Tell me what you thought about today. Tell me what you do when you're alone. What is it like to be you? What do you care about? What do you think about falafel? Do you like circuses? If you could be any animal, what animal would you be?"

Walking home from the pub, EV felt avid and awake. Her shoes, at the bottom of her legs, carried her home. Now she knew: I can say yes; I can say no.

Later, in her bathroom, while brushing her teeth, she had an accident, a fall. Her eyes opened to white grimed hexagonal tiles and red bleeding over shards of glass. Had her face shattered? Dizzy, she stood up and looked in the mirror.

His telephone number appeared in the phone book beside "P. Cornblum," but blood fell on the page and blotted it out. She had to call information and write the numbers out on her hand with a pen. Finally she heard the telephone ringing under her feet. "Allo?" he said, very distinctly. *Allo*. Where did he think he was?

"I think I've been shot in the head," she said. "Will you help me?" Even blurred and afraid, she took pleasure in having reason to disturb him.

He seemed surprised to see her. Through the red blur, EV saw the look on his face. "You weren't shot; you fell down drunk," he told her. He led her by the hand into the bathroom and showed her the red pool on the tile where she'd fallen on a pipe. "See the blood?" he said, pointing. "You fell here. You broke a glass. You have to go to the emergency room." He handed her a towel, then rooted in her closet and brought out black pants and an unfortunate gold stringy sweater that looked like gorilla fur. He exhumed her red shoes from the tangle of gleaming sheets on her futon. "Oh, Angel Feet, I won't ask why you sleep with your shoes," he said. He turned toward the window while she changed, and actually covered his face with his hands.

Like a date, he held her arm while they walked downstairs. EV held the towel against her eye. At the door to his apartment, she leaned against the wall outside while he put on his beige raincoat and chose a book to read. "What are you reading?" asked EV.

He turned the spine to her and she read the title, *Attitudes Toward His . . .* , before her eyes filled up.

In the street, a metallic mist sprayed down. P. Cornblum hailed a cab, guided EV into it, named a hospital and a route, then pulled bills from his wallet to pay.

At the hospital, he sat beside her with a clipboard in his lap and raindrops on the lenses of his glasses and asked personal questions: "Place and year of birth? Social Security number?" He filled in what he knew: her name, EV Hellman, which he'd seen on the mailbox, probably; her address, which was also his. EV drifted in her plastic seat, and told him everything he asked. She heard one of the nurses say into the telephone, "Plastic surgeon—Central Park South," and she jumped up. She walked stiffly to the desk, holding the towel against the damaged, leaking side of her face. "Can't you get somebody cheaper downtown?" she said.

Several nurses turned to EV, a glare of uniforms. "Insurance?" someone said.

"Do you take Visa?" EV asked.

Of course they took Visa.

"Do you have a Visa card?" EV asked P. Cornblum.

"Oh my *God,*" he said.

"Relax," EV assured him. She took hold of his cloth coat. "I'll pay you back from my security deposit."

A tiny smear of blood from her hand migrated to his sleeve and seemed to take him beyond horror. Then he laughed, a raucous bark. He handed over the clipboard and rummaged in his wallet.

A nurse wheeled EV away to a pink room, where eventually a man dressed in a nylon running suit appeared, a loaded syringe in one hand. EV's hand shot out to stop him. "You can't just stick a needle in," she said.

He took a step back, the needle poised in his hand. "Excuse me," he said. "I am Dr. Van. I just drove down from Fifty-ninth Street to sew up your face."

"You expect me to sit here and not react?"

"What kind of reaction were you planning?"

"You'll have to hold my arms down, something," she said.

Dr. Van smiled. "You want me to get your boyfriend in here to hold you down?"

"He's not my boyfriend," she said.

"I thought not."

Dr. Van called down the hall for a woman, who held EV's arms to her sides while he pricked and sewed. "You're lucky you got me and not some intern," he said. "This gash is an inch long—wreck your face."

"Will I have a scar?" she asked him.

"Of course you'll have a *scar,*" he said.

When he finished, he held up a mirror and showed her the black stitches from her eye to her cheek; they ended in two loose bristles near her ear. He handed her a pen and a square of yellow paper (a Post-it note!) and said, "Now, EV, put your phone number down here. If you turn out well, we can probably get this job written up in a magazine."

EV wrote down her name and telephone number. Dr. Van folded the note and slid it into the pocket of his running pants. He took her chin in his hand and turned her face this way and that, admiring his work. "Good, good. You should do something about that pink hair, though," he said. He winked at EV, strung a black patch over her damaged eye, then was gone.

The woman who'd pinned EV's arms rummaged in her pocket and handed over a piece of candy. EV said, "Thank you," and held the candy in her hand. The woman waited, but EV wouldn't be cowed. Even a small hard candy could unleash her appetite.

"I don't have insurance," she said. "But he put it on a credit card."

The woman shook her head. "I'm with Social Services," she said. "If you want to change your domestic situation, I can help."

"What would happen if I told you my boyfriend hit me?" EV asked.

The woman's hand moved close to the sleeve of EV's gorilla sweater. She looked as if she'd like to touch it. "Well," she said, "You can go to a safe house if you want. I can help you to get a restraining order. "

"Oh," said EV. "Well, he didn't hit me. We were having, you know, vigorous sex, and a painting fell off the wall."

The black patch over one eye ruined her sense of distance. EV walked carefully toward P. Cornblum, watching her feet move across the floor. The rain had left dark, destroying spots all over her red suede shoes.

"You look like picture day in hell," he said.

He guided her by both arms into a Yellow Cab, and they slid across the black vinyl seat.

"We could go somewhere and have a drink," EV suggested.

"Are you out of your mind?" he said.

The rubber tires sluiced through rainwater; then coins and paper money changed hands, the taxi door closed behind them and P. Cornblum's key turned in the lock. The soles of their shoes made scratching sounds on the tar paper the super had nailed to the stairs to protect the peeling linoleum. *Scratch, scratch, scratch*—like hens scrabbling in dirt.

He led the way. When they reached the third-floor landing, EV pinched the sleeve of his raincoat.

"If I'm quiet, can I come in for a minute?" she asked him.

The beige back of his raincoat softened, then hardened and squared. He turned around and faced her. There was no effort in his face, no effort at all; it was completely natural. She felt he might be on the verge of telling her some terrible truth she half-wanted to hear—but no. He crouched on the floor and pulled off her red shoes. The damp leather clung to EV's feet and then gave way suddenly as he threw the shoes—*bang* and *bang*—against the wall.

1972–1982

The Graduate

God held the line and Carole did not graduate. She was sent away, back home, presumably in disgrace. Later girls at Goode fared better. They studied abroad, won the chemistry prize and the Spanish prize, distinguished themselves at lacrosse, on violin. They marched for equal rights and equal pay, the right to consume birth-control pills and protest against nuclear power; they became treasurer and even head of class. They raised money for scholarships, organized and excelled. They ventured into the world, taught prostitutes in Central America to read, electrified villages in Africa, invented lucrative investment products on Wall Street. They entered the House and Senate, or raised children who did; they became cantors and neurologists.

Carole returned to Brooklyn, to her single working mother. It seemed to those she left behind like a vaguely terminal condition. Carole had had a chance; she'd thrown it away. Only Aileen Rebozos kept in touch with her and sent updates to *The Goodeman*. For an awkward year, Carole worked in some kind of shop. She held a tiny show of men's heads in a gallery—but in Brooklyn. She went abroad—to Paris and Ghana! Two years later, Mrs. Graves received a letter from Carole, curtly asking God for a recommendation and a transcript to be sent to the Rhode Island School of Design. God, by now miserably emeritus, wrote with grim pleasure of Carole's crimes against the school, her failure to graduate, the arrogance with which she'd occupied the new space that had been made for her—and for women of the future.

Carole wrote in her essay about being the only one, and then one of a very few of the first:

> It didn't matter so much that the Head was a sexist or a bigot or a snob, or basically uninterested in my testing him. That didn't harm me. I was used to it; I already had an aloof and absent father. God Byrd was just one person—a person he never had to question or think about—and I had more than one identity. How could that not be good? I had to decide on what relation I had to other people. Some people willed me invisible at Goode. I mean, the assumption was that we—students of color, girls—would simply assimilate. Nothing would really change. That was the point, wasn't it?
>
> My mother—she died this year of cancer—was ferocious, determined. And all her determination centered on me. It was what she gave me instead of affection, mostly. She didn't talk to me gently; she didn't ask what I wanted to do. She saw life as a struggle—that's why she sent me to a virtually all-white school. If it had been an all-white, no girls school forever, she would have been even more determined to send me there.
>
> At Goode, they repressed our true nature the way farmers stop watering their tomatoes, leaving the plants limp to swell the fruit. We were like that, "dirty girls" so parched and thirsty and stressed, it's strange our pencils didn't snap in two when we bit them. I don't remember critical thinking, logical inquiry, the quadratic equation, plane geometry, dactylic hexameter, Bernoulli's principle, the past participle of the verb *tenir,* the first element on the periodic table, the capital of Benin, the vice president under Taft, the rules of soccer, lacrosse or tennis, whether narcissism comes before or after the Oedipus complex, whether the prime rate goes up or down in a recession. What I remember is boys everywhere, like big white mice.

> I remember white men talking, talking, talking. No one asked about my experience as a human being. The Goode School was like a huge white skin that covered everyone—that covered me. My whole consciousness was black and poor and female every second of every day. The experience damaged, sharpened and defined me, and I would not trade it for anything.

After RISD, Carole went to Yale. She won prizes; her name turned up, sometimes attached to the Goode School like a burr on a wool scarf. She found a dealer and "turned out," as Mrs. Rebozos put it. That was the point, wasn't it? That Carole should carry with her the air and substance of entitlement, and a strong character. That she should "turn out," as if she had been white and wealthy, and a boy.

1982

The Ordination of Women

Pilgrim was perfect. Behind his metal-framed glasses he had blue lupine eyes, which hardened at the center to a bead. My daughter EV met him in New York. She sent me a picture of the two of them together, and right away I encouraged her to invite him up to Maidenhead. At my age, experience is like treasure saved up in the backs of drawers: Suddenly, you can't wait to give it all away to somebody who might use it.

EV resisted—but resistance is good. She sipped her coffee, which was all she'd take in the morning, and said, "Do I have to?"

Just a few years ago, EV was a chubby child. Now she weighs about eighty-five and eats practically nothing but hard candy and dry toast, though she still drinks. That's bad, I know, drinking with no vitamins going in, although thirst is a kind of hunger, which gives me hope. I'd thought a lover—like Pilgrim—might frankly say, "EV darling, a little flesh is useful in bed." This is hard to talk about. EV used to come home from school and put away cheese sandwiches and Little Debs; I spoke up then.

We drove to the airport together. EV asked if she could drive, and I said no, better not. The car's practically new, a headstrong Peugeot with barely seven thousand miles, and I know its temper best.

I suggested that we go early and stop for lunch at China Hill. "We could have a drink," I offered, in case she thought I was trying to force-feed her.

The last time I'd been there was six years ago, when EV was in high school. A doctor's office two towns over had called to confirm her appointment to get birth-control pills, and I offered to drive her—and buy lunch. That time, we drank a bottle of Blue Nun and ate sweet-and-sour chicken. I remember it as a highlight of our life—two hours of explicit mother-daughter talk. (I've got nothing new, but a good story improves, up to a point, with age.) It turns out EV had lost her virginity at fifteen—I was shocked and impressed to hear it—with her thirty-two-year-old math teacher in a trailer behind the general store, influenced by beer, distorted by fantasy, a fake-fur rug under her back, a mirror on the ceiling, the "older man" flattering and encouraging her. EV has always been competitive and eager to shock, but that's natural—we're so alike. I was glad she'd found a way to tell her story well.

This time, lunch was disappointing. I ordered a Manhattan and my favorite chicken dish with green peppers and maraschino cherries. EV had a glass of beer. She wouldn't eat anything, and worried that the sweet-and-sour sauce was all sugar that might put me into a coma on top of the vermouth and rye. She was right, of course, and I had to ask the waitress to box it all up. I asked some question about Pilgrim Cornblum—was he attentive, something like that—and she glared at me in such a way that my sweater, a hand-knit one I've always loved, suddenly sprouted legs that crawled over my skin. The sweater's no longer flattering—my neck is ropes and toggles—and I had on a white dickey, which had become constricting and hot. (We'd left Maidenhead in a fog, which burned off as we drove.) Just as I felt the betrayal of my favorite clothes, two gray-haired women came by our table. One of them said, "Excuse me, but all through lunch we wondered—are you an Episcopal priest?"

The Episcopal Church had just ordained four women in our county. I wondered myself where such women (pious, serious, perhaps sexually adventurous) had come from.

EV barked out a laugh.

"No?" said the woman who'd spoken first. "My friend thought not. I thought maybe. You know, a woman in a dickey."

"I am a French teacher at the public high school," I told them, noticing how the word *French* slightly brightened the leaden effect of the word *teacher*. I was used to that.

"You're French?"

"No." I was used to that, too.

"Well," said the friend, "sorry to interrupt your lunch."

"Not at all!" EV said, glad.

I'd allowed too much time, and we were early to the airport. EV drifted restlessly around the terminal in her awful acid green minidress, which exaggerated the boniness of her shoulders and knees. Her hair, dyed unrealistically, drew attention. I sat in a molded chair with my bag in my lap and waited for an hour, hating myself for not having brought a book to read. A board above the ticket counter said the plane was scheduled to arrive at 3:02. (The arrogant precision of the airline industry is one reason I don't fly.) Still, if all went well, we might be home by 4:30, not too early to get out the ice, the gin and the tonic water.

The plane touched down at 3:15. Somebody in an orange vest rolled a stair to the door, and I recognized Pilgrim from EV's description: "He's twenty-nine; he went to Yale." I wondered what this boy wanted with my daughter. He was perfect, short and round and pink—but perfect for what? He looked like a young God; I mean like Goddard Byrd might have looked in youth—fully formed, the clay still damp. I enjoyed him immediately. He was badly dressed in old, expensive clothes; he clearly felt no responsibility to be attractive. We see this often around Cape Wilde and Maidenhead—idle money wasted on the dowdy rich. Pilgrim looked down at the steps beneath him, completely unconscious of being met—of our eyes upon him. He looked forty, a pose. I recognized him at once as the kind of man who marries at thirty to relieve sexual strain (but does not marry a girl like EV), produces three children, loses hair, never pauses. An empire builder. Already he'd published a book on the history of systems. I wondered what they talked about, my daughter and this Pilgrim.

The barrier between us was made of sawhorses and plastic tape. If Pilgrim had looked up, he would have seen that EV's face expressed no particular joy or tenderness at the sight of him; she wanted more. At least I hoped she did. (I'd tried to raise a greedy, lusty girl—which EV so defiantly *was*, especially as a child.) In any case, for some men, a woman's esteem is not a factor, and Pilgrim's eyes remained on the sharp decline of the stair.

He kissed her on the mouth, which she allowed, and when that was done, EV wiped her lips and said, "Mei-Mei, this is Pilgrim. Pilgrim, this is Mei-Mei."

"Pleased to meet you," Pilgrim said, and held out his hand to be shaken.

"Enchantée," I said. I took the hand to my lips—a joke—and kissed it.

Pilgrim carried his luggage, one leather bag, and stowed it in back on the passenger side. EV opened the other rear door to sit in back. But then Pilgrim began to climb in back, too—to sit beside EV, as if I were a taxi driver! I thought it was a queer thing to do, worse than queer.

"Pilgrim, come sit shotgun with me," I said. "We'll give you the ride of your life."

Pilgrim looked alarmed.

"Her new car," EV explained.

"Oh, fine," he said.

I took charge, pointed out the beaver dams, the islands in the bay. "Smell the flats!" I told him as we crossed the bridge to town. I buzzed down all the windows and let in the phosphorescent odor of clams. Pilgrim was blind to the marvels of Cape Wilde—though he did seem drawn to EV, turning half-way around in his seat several times to make sure she was there, reaching a hand around to paw at her.

EV was so removed, I thought at first she might be reading. Since she'd come home from New York, we'd been on a Patricia Highsmith jag—long afternoons at the beach in our swimsuits, taking turns with *Ripley Under Water* or *Ripley Under Ground,* passing a bottle of baby oil and iodine between us, occasionally reading some choice bit out loud. I'd gotten out of her that Pilgrim was her downstairs neighbor in Greenwich Village. Amid the little intimacies and pressures of urban living, they'd become close.

"Are you reading something good, kitten?" I called to the rear, but before she could answer, Pilgrim said, "Nothing, actually, that I could recommend."

At home, he made no polite remarks about my treasures—the French clock, the life-size silver suit of armor I'd bought at an estate sale, wonderfully cheap. All of which I minded a little. He produced a bunch of spotty Dole bananas. "For the house," he said grandly, and put them in my hands.

"You'll have to bunk with EV," I told him. "There's no spare room."

"We'll manage," he said, and managed her down the hall. I heard beds being pushed together—those punishing twin beds with the ancient mattresses redolent of sour horsehair and EV's childhood emissions. I cracked ice into the bucket and watched through the back window as the starlings made their beeline into the birdhouse hole. I promised myself I wouldn't drink too much, would work for an hour before bed. I'd been meaning all summer to prepare some new exercises in *futur antérieur* and *plus-que-parfait.* At a certain level, my students feel a false sense of fluency. They live in the past and the present. It's important—not too soon and not too late—to introduce a subtler sense of time: what might be or should be, what will have been, what's over and done.

They came back for cocktails holding hands. EV still wore her funny green dress; she made gin and tonics for everybody. Pilgrim drank two and gobbled cheese and crackers. EV drank her gin quickly for a person who had eaten no lunch; she even scoffed up her lime.

EV's eating habits—if eating is still habitual for her—are a secret. I'm a lunch person; when EV visits, we usually "transcend supper," as she puts it, and make do with drinks and carrot sticks. I'd meant to defrost a lasagna in Pilgrim's honor but had forgotten. After an hour, it was still a hopeless brick. EV might have helped, suggested something—I can't imagine what.

"I have a lovely lasagna," I told them. "But it's cold."

Nevertheless, I drew Pilgrim out, over our drinks, about systems and history. We spoke of busing in Boston; he was, it turned out, all for it. "That's because, of course, you went to private schools," I ventured, and Pilgrim laughed. I'd asked EV about it earlier, just to be sure. He'd gone to Loomis before Yale.

By 7:30, Pilgrim had begun to suffer and starve. Crackers and cheese don't quell the appetites of men like him, who expect to be well fed, who see regular meals as a form of discipline.

He and EV sat together on the cat-clawed love seat in the living room. Pilgrim's khaki leg touched EV's naked one and his hand rode high above her knee. His eyes were hard to read through his muddy glasses, though they *looked* bold—challenging me. But to what?

Finally he said, "Let me take you both out for dinner." EV contracted at the mention of food.

"You two go," I said. "Take him to the fish fry, kitten."

"Oh, for God's sake," EV said. But I knew exactly what he wanted.

"You get good fish—from the ocean—here," he said.

"That's exactly right," I told him.

Pilgrim grabbed EV's hand and said, "I'm hungry."

I'd forgotten the claim a man's needs have over a woman. I stood up and said, "I'm feeling peckish, too."

First, EV wanted to change. She went off; then I heard her calling, and went to see. She came out of her closet with a pair of blue jeans and unfurled them over the bed. "What are these?" she said.

"Your blue jeans, darling," I told her. "You wore them every day in high school."

"I never wore these! These aren't those," she said.

"They do look big for you," I said carefully.

She poked at the legs. "These were never mine."

"Darling, I think you should go look at yourself. I think you should step on the scale and weigh yourself."

"Look at my*self*!" EV was beside herself. "I can't stand this."

"You mean Pilgrim, darling?"

"I don't want him here. There's something wrong with him," she said, her eyes wild.

"There is nothing *wrong* with him," I said. "Now go find some clothes you don't mind getting fishy, and wash your face. We will meet you outside."

I walked out of the room, turned the corner and found Pilgrim lurking. "EV's just changing," I told him. "Why don't we wait on the porch?"

We watched a bat circling the yard. "Do you have the time?" I asked, and he showed me the platinum face of his watch.

"I can't see anything that small," I said.

"Seven-thirty-eight," said Pilgrim.

When EV emerged, still wearing her terrible green dress, she said we should go without her, that she had a headache. Something defiant radiated around her, something shrill. Pilgrim had seen it before; I could tell.

"We could all just stay here," I said. "I could boil you an egg, Pilgrim."

"I don't want an egg," said Pilgrim. "I want real food."

"Of course you do," I told him.

"So you two go," EV said.

The idea sounded reasonable and civilized. We'd go, Pilgrim and I—without EV—to the Friday fish fry and eat together. We'd feed.

"Will you be our driver?" I asked him.

"Pilgrim doesn't drive," EV said.

"I *can* drive," Pilgrim said.

"Mei-Mei never lets anybody drive her precious car," EV said.

"That's not true," I said, and handed him the keys.

Friday night at the fish fry is packed and steamy. We sat in a booth in back, across from each other on the red leatherette.

"We'll drink wine?" Pilgrim asked.

"That would be fun," I said.

He looked over the list—I'd never seen a wine list at the fish fry—and ordered a bottle of Pouilly-Fuissé. I perked up at the French. Debbie O'Greefe brought the wine and two wine-glasses, which gleamed in the greasy light.

I barely recognized Debbie at first. She'd run to fat a little bit, which was too bad. Debbie was a student of mine once, a classmate of EV's. Her mother was our landlady, my husband's and mine, years and years ago—a tragic figure. Remarkably, she once had her own nipple sewn onto her forehead after her awful husband severed it in a so-called act of love. I used to use her as a local example when I taught English and we read *The Scarlet Letter.*

"Ça va bien, Debbie?" I asked her.

Debbie blew out an embarrassed little laugh. *"Oui?"* she said, as if it were a question. (How could it not be? Twenty-two, just EV's age, and the poor girl had three children.) She struggled with the cork for a minute, then poured out wine. Pilgrim's glass touched mine. *"Cin-cin,"* he said.

"Choo-choo," I said. The wine was very good, dry and almost puckery. It had an old-world heaviness I liked. Pilgrim sniffed away at his glass.

"Lovely wine, Debbie," I said. *"Un bon vin blanc."* We used that phrase in French classes to practice vowels, and I thought Debbie would recognize it. But she only looked uncomfortable, as if I were speaking in tongues. She smiled tightly and pocketed her corkscrew.

"I'll be back," she said.

"So you're a French teacher," Pilgrim said. "Done that long?"

"A thousand years," I told him.

"Do you go to France and so on?"

"I've never been. I don't fly. EV went last year. With a man."

"Shouldn't you go," he said, "for your work?"

"I have no desire—no need," I said. "There's no professional pressure, and I don't push myself too hard. You'd probably say this is a two-bit kind of town."

"Why teach French if you don't care about the culture, the people?"

"I don't teach French because of the culture or the people," I said. "Fourteen years ago, the school needed someone and I came forward. I never pretended to be French. I do love the language—the grammar, the literature—and I like my job. I think travel is overrated. People are the same everywhere, don't you think?" Discreetly, I pressed two fingers to my heart to sop up a drizzle of moisture.

Debbie returned with her pad, and I ordered steamed clams

to start, a salad to share, and two fish frys. Pilgrim tied a plastic bib around his neck. We talked of his research in Boston, where he'd studied "systems and history." He was at work on a book about integration and busing in the early 1970s. I raveled out my stories about Goode and God, the early days of coeducation there, as well as my own narrow escape from that doll's house. He seemed politely interested, maybe more; in the moment, I felt I had something concrete to offer him. I told him that I always thought of Boston as my city, too, since some of my life had happened there. Pilgrim made one generous remark. He said, "I think that to know a city, you can't just live there; you have to visit it."

It was a beautiful thing to say—and so true. I thought of one time when EV was at Smith (a scholarship girl) and I drove across the state in my old car, my beloved unheatable Escort, to visit. I wore two pairs of long underwear and socks and kept a hot-water bottle in my lap the whole way. I got a room—quite seedy, but cheap and in town. Every day I walked for miles. EV was busy and I barely saw her, except one afternoon when I sat for some portraits she did for her photography class. It was more than enough just to know she was there. But then I came down with a cold and decided to leave early. I drove to Boston and took a room at the Parker House—an outrageous extravagance. The next day, I walked around the city, sneezing and feverish, into the State House, where the sacred cod still hangs on the wall, and into the new outdoor market, where I saw an old man plunge the blue numbers on his forearm into a barrel of brine and pull up an enormous, reeking pickle. I walked by the address of the first apartment I shared with my husband, Heck, though the neighborhood had long since been swallowed up by the university's hospital. Revisiting it all, I felt like a stranger, an outsider, seeing the place in its strangeness, reliving moments that felt like nothing twenty years ago, when I'd thought there would be more.

I reached over the bread and wine and plucked Pilgrim's glasses from his nose. He seemed blind without them, but he didn't try to stop me. I dipped the glasses in my tumbler of water and wiped them clean on a paper napkin. The metal frames suggested the influence of Benjamin Franklin or John Lennon. When I slid the glasses back on Pilgrim's nose, he looked as if clear vision changed his view. "Wow, Mei-Mei," he said. "You don't really look like anyone's mom."

"Thanks, Pilgrim."

I thought of EV, who would now be standing at the refrigerator, trolling for scraps of food, filling herself with remorse.

Debbie O'Greefe brought the clams and two bowls of butter and broth. "I've never had these before," Pilgrim said.

"Clams?" I said. "That's extraordinary, as you're from Connecticut."

"Jewish mother," he said.

"How did you come to be called Pilgrim, then?"

"My father was an asshole."

I detached the veil from the neck of one and dipped it into his butter. Then I lifted it to his mouth, pushed my fingers through his lips and laid it on his tongue.

"Good?" I asked him. He gave me a long, assessing look, which I allowed. I've never minded being looked at.

"Very good," he said.

I fed him another.

"Go on," I said.

Pilgrim removed the veils from one clam at a time and laid them all in the butter bowl. When he'd finished, he popped the clams straight into his mouth. Butter drizzled down his chin, his bib. When he'd finished, his glasses were filthy again. He pushed them up on his nose. "Ah, the finger bowl!" he said, and plunged his hands in the broth.

Debbie brought our fish—elegant haddock. Under the breading, the fish is white and tender. You can eat all you want, but I limit myself to one piece, and another to take home for lunch. EV and I used to go every Friday night back in the days when EV ate food and we never thought of wine with dinner. The fish comes in a red plastic basket lined with waxed paper to hold the oil. They send out french fries, too, but I taught EV never to get involved with those.

Pilgrim, though, was no product of mine. Let him eat them. He ate quickly, with an intellectual attention, and spoke only to call to Debbie for more haddock. The table filled with red plastic baskets and balled-up paper napkins. When Debbie finally tore the green ticket off her pad, she couldn't find a free space on the table, so I took it from her swollen fingers. "Thank you, Debbie. This is mine, Pilgrim. It's delicious to have you with us."

He nodded, seemed pleased with that.

The evening was warm and the street busy with people coming out of the restaurants, dazed from their big dinners. I suggested that we stop and buy a bag of penny candy for EV.

Lolly's is the place. It's been there since I was a girl, when a candy really cost a penny, and old Mrs. Lolly stood behind the glass cases, tall and extremely serious, and waited with her metal tongs while we chose. "One cigarette, one slice of coconut bacon, one chocolate soldier, two lemon slices—no, one lemon slice and one orange slice . . ." EV and I used to walk over after the fish fry and split a little bag. Lolly's has new candies now, raspberries and blackberries, and tiny, perfect bananas and peas.

"I'd rather buy her ice cream," he said.

"Don't you know her *at all*?" I asked him.

He put his hands in his pockets and went sullen. The pleats in the front of his khaki slacks cradled his little tummy.

"You're just wrong about the ice cream," I said. "EV never eats it."

"She eats ice cream with me," he said. "I feed it to her on a spoon. In bed."

My ears rang a bit. "Why are you telling me this?" I asked him.

"Did I go too far? I thought you two discussed all your exploits together," he said.

"As a matter of fact, no, we don't."

I left him there, walked a block up to Lolly's, pushed the door open and jangled the bell.

Who loved my daughter best? The then-narrow, hungry face of Debbie O'Greefe came to mind. I used to come home exhausted after school—Mrs. O'Greefe marginally "watching" the girls—and come upon the scene of an orgy: buttery toast crumbs, balled-up napkins, a bag of Oreos torn open on the counter next to two glasses containing the dregs of grimy-looking milk. How could they be so hungry? Once I found a "Resipy for an Explosive" scribbled down in EV's pretty handwriting and atrocious, below-grade-level spelling. The brew included "Baking soda, Lyons milk, erbs, oyel, licker and seedlings," all congealing together in a Pyrex bowl. More chilling was this note: "I luv u EV," surrounded by hearts impaled with arrows. I discouraged that friendship in guilty, subtle ways. I wished that I were a fairer, better person. I wished Debbie O'Greefe were the kind of child I could have loved—a biracial child, for example, or an Indian.

I spent $3.75 on a medium-size bag. Even penny candy isn't sold by the piece anymore; it's sold by the pound in big self-service bins with plastic scoops. We are a nation of gluttons.

When I came out, Pilgrim was standing on the sidewalk, holding a freezer bag from the fancy summer-only grocery; I've never even stepped in there. He said, "I'm sorry. I shouldn't drink."

"It's perfectly all right," I said. "I shouldn't have said EV went to France with a man. That was indiscreet."

"I won't tell."

We walked peacefully to the car. Pilgrim pulled the keys out of his pocket and opened the passenger door for me. But once behind the wheel, he was lost.

"Take a right here," I told him, and sent him up Whalebone Neck, past the big old houses there—most of them undermaintained, rotten really, unoccupied even in this high season. He drove badly, though not, I thought, from the wine. High and nervous, I sat in the unfamiliar passenger seat of my new car. Pilgrim was brittle, his glasses greasy; he could crash.

I put a hand on his leg and squeezed.

He drove off to the side of the road, away from the streetlights, down into a grassy ditch under a maple tree—I assumed we were having an accident—and stopped the car. He unfastened his seat belt, then mine, leaned over and kissed me on the mouth. There was nothing exploratory or sensory about the kiss. It was all transmission, no reception; he might have been having a convulsion on my face. He unbuttoned the front of my blouse, or tried to. I thought of the beautiful French word for confusion: *brouilliamini.* I sprang the little hook in front of my bra and Pilgrim released a childish noise—a whine of frustration or anguish or complicated pleasure. I stroked his head, his thinning baby hair. His hands moved awkwardly to the fly of his pants, which he worked to unbutton.

This was all over very quickly, almost before I understood how minor was my role. He mopped himself with a wad of tissues he extracted from the box I keep between the seats, then crushed the tissues into a ball. He had to turn on the ignition, of course, to buzz the electric window down. The Peugeot roared to life and he tossed the ball—it looked exactly like a snowball—across the street and onto the lawn of the now-defunct historical society, where it lay all summer like some unseasonal marvel, glowing on the grass.

⁓

EV hadn't bothered to switch on the porch light. The chime on the door pinged anxiously when I opened it. The house was dark, though a small light shone from the kitchen. "We're home, darling!" I called.

EV wandered down the hall toward us. She'd put on an ancient robe of mine, a kimono I bought on sale at Filene's before she was born. "You both reek of wine and fried things," she said.

"Pilgrim found French wine at the fish fry. Can you imagine?"

"I brought us ice cream," Pilgrim said, squeezing EV's arm.

"And *I* brought penny candy. Those little berries you like!" I rattled the paper bag in front of her face.

Reaching for the bag, EV looked like a child again, small, greedy and expectant, though of these qualities, she was really only small. I wondered whether I had ever been a good mother to her, and how, under different circumstances, I might have been a better one.

2004

Himself

He had no way of cleaning himself *out,* God admitted when pressed by Dr. Hauk. He hadn't ever paid much attention to himself. How could he get under the skin? He shed flakes.

He'd lost a lung to tuberculosis after the war, a few teeth. This last was just a flap, a scrim. But he would be different without it. He stood in the WC and inspected himself, took himself in his hand.

No need for an operation, Hauk assured him, just a procedure. (But then Hauk died, and God had to see the new man, Wu.)

God understood that the procedure would change him slightly forever. Circumcision would fundamentally alter the narrow peninsula God thought of as himself. He dreamed he'd become monstrous, womanly, his body covered with nipples. In horrified fascination, dreaming, he touched them. Then it was as if a presence held him down, as if a body lay on his. He tried to sit up, but he was paralyzed, dozing. The Presence pressed on him; he pushed back. The Presence, having made her point, withdrew. God stood up, wiped a trail of salt from his chin and looked into the smoky, pockmarked mirror on the wall, a glass so ancient, it no longer reflected anything. The mirror was a formality; God knew what he looked like. He opened his mouth to smile and one of his teeth, canine, fell with a tiny clatter to the floor. Ashamed, he secreted it away in the pocket of his pants and lay for the rest of the afternoon in his chair like a spider in its web, shaking a bit, but working nonetheless, trolling for a beginning to the story of his life. Or had he written that part down already, the history?

The next morning, Mrs. Graves rapped her knuckles on the door—the bathroom door. "What are you getting up to in there, Mr. Byrd?" she asked. "We have to get to the HOM, the HMO."

He cleared his throat. "Not the HMO—it's the Veterans Hospital."

"Oh hell!" she said, and beat her fist against the wall.

He looked at himself. He put himself back in his shorts. Then he buttoned up his pants and went out with Mrs. Graves to her little Toyota. When he'd told her the car service wanted forty-seven dollars, she'd insisted on driving him herself. The figure outraged them both; they would suffer the ride.

The Veterans Hospital stood on a hill overlooking the industrial corridor, accessible via the Veterans Parkway—a narrow river of fast-moving traffic. The VA Hospital reminded God of the war, which had been beautiful and terrible; he had helped to liberate Shanghai.

Mrs. Graves settled into a plastic chair in the waiting area with a magazine. A nurse led God to an examination room and gave him a johnny to put on. When she returned a few minutes later, he was still standing there, wearing his raincoat, with the johnny over one arm, absorbed in a diagram of renal functions. She turned away while he undressed, then folded his slacks over the back of the chair and helped him up to the examination table; he lay back immediately with a kind of crash. She set a paper cup of orange juice down on a tray beside his head and left him alone.

God put his hand on himself and held himself. He protected himself with his hand. The door opened suddenly and God's hand shot up.

"You should be feeling fairly relaxed, Mr. Byrd," said a nurse he couldn't see over his chest.

"Should I?"

"Oh yes. The pill will be taking effect any minute. Do you want to look at a magazine?"

"No!" he shouted back. "We're fine as we are."

The knife rose bloody in Dr. Wu's hand. God bellowed—he roared. Who would have known the old man had so much feeling in him? He squeezed his eyes shut, but pain bled into him and he rose up—a monster, roused.

Mrs. Graves waited, stiff-lipped, impressed by his sounds, which traveled into the waiting room and made *Time* magazine tremble in her lap. Everyone pretended not to hear it. Mrs. Graves looked down at the article before her—about syndicate-made pop stars from Fabian to the Monkeys and the new hip-hop music by Sugarhill Gang and Grandmaster Flash and the Furious Five, which put back what rock took out—words—and changed how one thought of rebel music.

At the cashier's, he collapsed on the linoleum and hit his head on the desk. While she wasn't looking, someone put him into a wheelchair. Mrs. Graves pulled out wads of money—tens, twenties, change—and flung it all down on the counter. The charge was only five dollars; he was a veteran.

"He shouldn't be disoriented like this," a nurse said accusingly to Mrs. Graves. "I gave him a Seconal in his orange juice."

"Do you need a taxi?" one of the attendants asked.

"That's ridiculous," said Mrs. Graves. "I have a car.

"We'll get you home and you'll feel better," she told God.

"What do you know about it?" he cried out. The margins of his eyes were dull yellow, the blue pupils metallic and scattered.

An orderly wheeled him to the car and put him in. Mrs. Graves wrapped a seat belt around his tan raincoat. She turned the key in the ignition and nosed the car toward the edge of the parkway, a hideous snake of red lights. Cars veered sickeningly away, their horns unfurling like ribbons of sound.

"I hate this section," Mrs. Graves remarked. "I take the back roads when I can."

We are dead, God thought. He moaned with agony—and relief.

Somehow, she got them home alive. She bustled in the kitchen with cans of chowder and Indian pudding. God sat on a straight-backed chair, still in his raincoat.

"I've never heard anyone scream so loudly," she told him cheerfully. "No one could read. I pretended to have nothing to do with you."

God wheezed out a sound of anguish.

"I've never heard such carrying-on! The nurse gave you a pill."

"She gave me nothing but orange juice."

"The pill dissolves *in* the orange juice."

"I was in no position to drink orange juice. I was lying down."

Mrs. Graves softened, turned and put a hand on God's arm. "You poor man," she said. "It's horrid to lose any part of yourself. I don't care how old we are."

The procedure cleared something that had blocked him. Overnight, groaning in his bed, God saw that the whole structure must be different; he and his kind must cut the cord. He had been a prisoner behind a wall, crouched in a tormenting position, nourishing the wall umbilically, as it were, with the juice of his life. Or did he feed from the wall? The meaning of life had come to him passively. He had taken the motto of others directly to heart—The Unexamined Life Is Not Worth Living—had examined nothing on his own. Everything he thought he knew, the contents of his head, what he thought of as himself (as much "himself" as the friendly appendage so recently having gone under the knife) was like a turtle in its shell. He had never broken free, had never suffered the prick of an original thought. His head was a prison, his bones a cage. He let out a slow breath and exhaled words—small black typewritten lines that looked like ants, marching up and out of the depths of him, carrying *stuff*—the crumbs of other men. He breathed again and saw the tiny black specks organize themselves into recognizable letters—*are we not drawn onward we few drawn onward to new era*—before they broke up and faded out.

He'd been crouched behind his wall, holding it up so that others might slip their prayers between the stones. He'd been part of a great machine—first as a student, then as a teacher and then, finally and for a few generations, as the Head. How many boys had he produced to specifications he had lain awake in the night improving, refining? How many articles had he contributed to *The Independent School Journal*? "If a man wants to maintain that state of white heat necessary to transmit the essence of great works to his students, how he can maintain it on distant recollection, I do not know." How sternly he had believed in himself! He had put that fire into every boy he could; he'd taught them that these poems, these rhythms, these meters, these themes, these characters were better than all the rest. How did he know? Who had told him? What if he'd been wrong?

He'd studied Greek as a boy because the democratic values of ancient Athens endured in Cape Wilde; so many boys were trained to endure them. Now the era of the old, narrow, ossified, privileged, entitled few—the men who had risen up, like himself, in the great liberal tradition—had ended. He was an old man now and had nothing important left to lose. Without his foreskin, he felt exquisitely sensitive, receptive, even. Before she left him, his wife, Madeline, had lost a toe, poor girl. Then she died, he wouldn't see her anymore. His own venerable flap was now nothing but a dry rose petal.

Toward morning, he dreamed of death. He found himself unprepared, having forgotten to bring a pair of socks from his top drawer, where his good nine-toed wife used to tuck them, rolled up into themselves. And so he had to stand barefoot in purgatory with other forgetful old men. What a disappointing end. He'd imagined light—if not a blaze of glory, a small persistent glow.

2005

The Death of God

Mrs. Graves tended God with professional solicitude. She cooked light meals, digested the newspaper and regurgitated small nuggets for his benefit. She ran the laundry and the vacuum and took the recycling to the curb. Recycling! God had not heard of it, but his interest almost immediately gave way to a sense of mastery, and he took charge of separating the cans, bottles and paper goods. During this period, Mrs. Graves also put God's obituary into her laptop. Now it would never have to be retyped. She showed him how she would send it to all the newspapers in advance; the date of his passing could be added later.

"You forgot to mention your ex-wife, Madeline," she remarked loudly after she read his draft. "I put her in."

Mrs. Graves worked as efficiently as a machine. At times, she became almost too interested in her work, and impatient with his interference. She couldn't help going under, submerging. She told his story the way a prophet speaks: by seeing. (His voice came to her through a sort of catheter tube to her brain.) As his secretary for twenty-five years, she felt she knew him better than anyone, certainly better than he knew himself. She had read the 133 legal pads that formed the foundational documents of his life story; indeed, he had forced the pages upon her with all the implications in that phrase of urgent physicality, until finally she'd said, "Enough already," and climbed the stairs with his legal pads and her laptop, leaving him at the base station.

Like most literary characters, God wasn't exactly the figure he imagined. Mrs. Graves spent several hours a day—pacing, transcribing, composing—in a fever, really, of creation. She'd experienced nothing like it for years: that degree of engagement with another human being, that degree of control.

A scale, like the patterns on the skin of reptile, covered his head, his forearms and his shins. His handkerchiefs were rags with monograms so ancient, their hand-sewn letters had unraveled. Cataracts muddied his view. He hadn't been the same since the circumcision; Mrs. Graves had said herself it was too late in life to make that kind of change. While she worked, he sat on the manila folder kept prophylactically under his usual seat on the couch to catch any residual drizzle. He still enjoyed music and rose every morning at five to play his piano in the basement. Occasionally, he fell—he confessed it—but so far had managed to pick himself up again. He often dozed or even slept in his chair, to avoid confrontations with the furniture. Sometimes she came or went and found him so far removed from consciousness, she thought he might be dead, but then she heard a low roar within, like a furnace firing.

Loss was one theme: the headship of the school, the battle over girls, memory, prostate, lung, teeth, foreskin. After Shanghai, he'd spent six months in a TB ward in a suburb near the capital. That was the year he wrote down his impressions and began the log of life he'd kept up ever since. In that lost year, he'd outlined his obsessions and made his original list of one hundred necessary books. To avoid obvious omissions, he'd polled the other men in the ward, but found their tastes ephemeral, populist. Madeline had written letters from home, which did not survive, but to which God faithfully had replied. ("I feel an unprecedented need to unfurl and expose and impress myself on the page.") He'd made a note, "Please save," on every one, and Mad had saved them all.

Who could read it all? Who would protect those who'd be hurt by whatever he'd written? You couldn't drop 133 legal pads into the recycling, another reason old men needed younger wives to outlive and clean up after them, dispose of their lives gradually. Who cleaned up after the women? Mrs. Graves, for one, had already cleaned up after herself.

He could die at home; she'd stay by his side. She knew how to keep him comfortable; give him a few hours a day to review the contents of his busy head, then knock him back again. She'd burn the papers in small batches in the evenings in the cozy fireplace upstairs.

Mrs. Graves sipped a glass of beer and read:

> I went birding Sunday afternoon with the Sapphist, Mrs. X. We tromped around Wilde Hill with binoculars in the kind of companionable silence I had known heretofore only with men. A silence adequate and rich enough to bind us two together on a path, counting birds, communicating with nods and grunts at some force of nature, an oriole or a grebe. Most women have no interest in the world, are bored by bird migrations and Mercator projections and the movement of machines. They prefer to dilate about human behavior. There is no contact they will not force to a crisis by speaking. The subtle world is scattered to the wind in the zealous sweep of women's chatter. But with this manly birder I felt free.

She sat in the bonny nook, reading God's life, which took her more deeply into her own life, into moments of strong feeling.

This is why we read, she thought, to disappear—then disappeared. Sometimes God called out to Mrs. Graves and could not rouse her.

Other times, she'd lean over the banister and call down, "Would you care for another glass of gin, Mr. Byrd?"

He would. He allowed himself to fade back into the shadows that played at the back of his mind: the legions of boys, those doomed foot soldiers!—playing their hands of poker on the poke boat at Chongqing, the dead man floating on the yellow river. God woke feeling responsible, drooling silver trails of salt.

The publications office had asked Mrs. Graves to help put God's notebooks into some order, preferably thirty-nine pages to be printed (the type transferred from a plate to a rubber blanket, then to vellum) in the same process the school had used for every biography of every head since the introduction of the offset printing press in 1903. They wanted it all in time for graduation, having waited patiently for over twenty-five years. It moved God deeply that Mrs. Graves, so late in life, would continue pro bono to do what she had always done for him.

Mrs. Graves worked tirelessly in the bonny nook, with its India-rubber desk, its view of the ocean and the trees, its shelves of books by men, its Colonial braided rug. In spite of lumbar complaints, a squeaking hip, the shocking sense that she might never again have sex with another person, well, Mrs. Graves had learned to love herself. She also took an almost sensual pleasure in the act of writing God, creating him.

God enjoyed the familiar sound of a woman banging at a keyboard, working on his behalf with unnatural diligence. It reminded him of marriage, the distaff side.

With Mrs. Graves to help with the typing and shaping, it was natural that the work would—at last—come to an end.

With every word she wrote, he died a little. He slept poorly, felt bored into by worms too small to see, pinpricks in his skin. Specks fell from his eyelashes and burrowed in his blanket.

He stared at the backs of his spotted hands as if they belonged to another man he wondered about. Those same hands shook as he read from a sheaf of papers she'd printed out for him.

He had lived, as the Chinese proverb has it, in interesting times. Born near the dawn of the century, he had come of age toward the end of the first war. In the second war, he'd helped to liberate Shanghai. (The dead man floated by on a drift of muddy water in his dreams.) Being among the dead had changed him, and made him more alive—a saved man. He survived the Great Depression, the crisis of modernism, civil rights, integration, McCarthy, the Bay of Pigs, the 1960s, black power, the sexual revolution, Vietnam and the Cold War! Yet still he felt connected to his boy's spirit and body, his hand on the tiller of a daysailer off Penzance Point on a wet and breezy afternoon, alone with the bay swelling and yielding beneath him like some sea monster—or a woman.

"Where did you get this?" he asked her. She had invaded his head, his thoughts, his memories. Grateful, he wept.

"Oh, I've transcribed and assembled, but the story of the century—well, others have been there, too." She patted him on the shoulder, softened. "Would you care for another glass of gin, Mr. Byrd?"

He paused, thinking. Mrs. Graves soldiered on, her still-nimble fingers quietly pushing down the keys, her face expressionless, professional and without judgment. A small fish sandwich lay untouched in a tea saucer on the arm of her chair. His old friend, his old ally—what was she, really? He understood that life as he knew it would not be possible without the benevolent energy of women. Fried bacon, clean sheets, cream cheese and olive sandwiches, picnics, travel abroad, sock drawers, fresh, typed pages, Meals on Wheels. And yet her very diligence irritated him.

"You are still typing," God remarked finally. "I've stopped speaking, but you are still typing."

She turned her impenetrable brown eyes toward him. "I haven't finished," she said.

But then she never finished. She lost her way. The manuscript she'd prepared over the course of several months gradually lost coherence and strayed from the main themes:

> O, God, careless old man too busy to notice how time ate you up. Your velvet chair reeked of an old man's pee and the old mink coat in the bedroom shed like a horse. Your ties turned yellow and coffee spattered your cream-colored coat like blood on a wall. I loved your cloudy blue eye looking beyond the wisteria vine, unblinking, as coolly as if Death were the nurse who drew your bath.

When did she slip? She'd continued to drive, and to drop off Meals on Wheels to other elderly people. God did not detect the change until one afternoon (past time for the glass of gin she customarily offered) he went to the bonny nook and found her standing with her legs wide apart on the floor, urine streaming between them. "Oh, horrible! Horrible!" she said.

Her work habits had remained steady and she typed much of every day, but when God happened to look at a page she'd written, he saw that her transcriptions had become mechanical:

> ajasjdkjlkjrjeurjkfksdkfnsijrkfksjhfskjhkjhjhak

Her lawyer sold her house and antiques, and then called in the junk dealer and an ambu-van from the long-term-care facility. Childless, her ex-husband long gone, Mrs. Graves had for years paid a premium on end-of-life insurance to assure she would never be a burden to anyone.

EV stands under the lavender wisteria, the hoary vine. She rings the bell and, to hell with it, opens the door. The rubber tree, oppessed these many years by the ceiling, has curled back upon itself, and died finally. The grandfather clock ticks once a second. EV stands in a silvery spray of dust motes and takes it all in. She sets her canvas duffel bag down by the door and moves toward the human sounds coming from the downstairs bedroom. She approaches the door and finds the enormous form of God, groaning and raving—apparently sleeping.

"You can't go in there," an old woman calls out. "Mr. Byrd is resting."

"Mrs. Jones?" EV asks.

"Yes. I'm with Skilled Care."

"I am EV Hellman."

"Ah, you came," says Mrs. Jones. She plucks at the ragged half of a sandwich she's brought from the bedroom and takes a bite.

"Come with me to the kitchen, dearie. We'll have a cup of tea. He wakes at four for his cocktail. You can see him then."

The grandfather clock struck the hour—four. And there she stood, EV Hellman, in the doorway. She held in one hand a leather bag with metal handles. A bit of metal glinted in one nostril. He had not seen her for five years. She'd given reasons—San Francisco, New York. "Ahoy," she said, as if she were a passenger boarding a ship, avoiding, as she always had, the awkwardness of calling him by some name. She put down the bag and came forward. He felt the tension of a woman advancing even as he anticipated her embrace.

She helped him to his feet. God stood beside her, unsteady, taller than she was. EV had always seemed stunted by the cold. She claimed to have grown two inches when, at the age of eighteen, she moved away from Cape Wilde.

"You'll have to buss me on the mouth," God told her. "I feel nothing."

"Moi," she said loudly, and kissed it.

His pants leg had ridden up beyond the band of one sock, revealing reptilian scales. He understood the commanding impression he made of age and wear, his venerable presence in the ancestral home. Sunlight hit the wide pine boards on the floor, which were beautifully worn down by years. The dirt between the boards had turned to a gleaming black wax, and the familiar furnishings remained where they had lived since before he was born: Aunt Olympia's rubber tree pressing at the ceiling, his grandfather's clock, the mahogany furnishings with their velvets and fleur-de-lis—all of it, he saw now, begrimed and shabby. "Mrs. Graves helped keep up appearances," he said. "But now she's gone."

"I'll put down my bag and wash my face," EV said. "Then I'll mix us a drink, if you're still allowed to have one."

"I was cleared by Dr. Hauk—before he died—to have two. It's the best hour of the day."

"Put your bag upstairs," he called after her, "in my room."

"Why?" she asked, registering alarm.

"I sleep down here."

"Oh, right," she said.

"You'll find clean sheets on the bed," he called after her.

She turned around to look at him. "You made a bed?" she asked.

"Mrs. Graves put sheets on the bed before she . . . retired."

He heard the girl upstairs in the bath, squeezing off the old tap with the pliers he kept on the sink. She descended almost immediately, disappeared into the kitchen and brought back two glasses on a tray. Holding a glass challenged God's stamina, his fingers had so little feeling in them. She'd found the gin—under the kitchen sink with the cleaning-out equipment—and mixed martinis. She handed God one; ice rattled pleasantly. He leaned forward and touched her glass with his. "Your health," he said.

"Cin-cin," she said. The first sip, promising. He put down his drink and laid his hands on his knees.

She went out again and brought back crackers and cheese on a plate that bore an etching of the Goode School chapel in red. "Don't break that," he warned her a bit sharply. (He'd promised himself he would not *shout* at her.) She moved a manila envelope from its place on the seat of the couch to the table in front of her and set down her drink. "Tell me about your health," she said. He pointed an ear in her direction and made her say it again.

"Defanged!" he told her. "Castrated!"

They drank peacefully for a few minutes. "Remind me," he said, "how you and I are connected."

"You and my mother, Mei-Mei Hellman, and I—we lived here the year—the year the Goode School let in girls. Do you remember? I used to bring you the ice water from the urinal. I used to sleep in the bonny nook. My father was Heck Hellman. He was a student of yours at Goode."

"Heck Hellman! Hum!" said God, and his eyes filled with tears. "And you were one of those Goode girls, were you?"

"No, my mother taught in the public schools. I went to Wilde High."

"Very good."

He'd gathered some books that dated from Olympia's and even his grandfather's time: Gisborne's *An Enquiry into the*

Duties of the Female Sex, Darwin on female education, Whytt on nerves, Smith's *Midwifery,* Hayes on coughs and colds, Niles on original sin, Terence's *Comedies,* Lewis and Clark's *Travels,* Hutchinson's *History of Massachusetts,* Charles Knowlton's *Fruits of Philosophy* from 1832—from which God had gleaned useful, gripping facts about the sexes. There was also his father's copy of the King James Version, and Pringle's *Observations on the Diseases of the Army.* He didn't need them anymore.

"That's kind of you," she said doubtfully.

He was writing a book himself, he confided, his blue eyes narrowing.

"I've heard about that," she said.

"It's a history," he told her, "of the ocean and the trees."

He slept on the fusty bed downstairs and dreamed of illicit loves. *Dear Mrs. Rebozos, my sweet gynecomaniacal saint, let us not to the marriage of true minds admit impediment! My bride no longer finds me lovable—the rugged breath of age is upon me. . . .* And he pressed her gently up against the open window and the scent of Parker House rolls and his bay rum, using his experience and expertise (though both had been called into question) to introduce sensations into her rather brittle body. Even in the dream he had to overlook a coolness coming off the skin. Pressing into her was like pressing into a balloon—some fragile, almost infinitely flexible but still definite boundary. When he finished, a breeze came up through the window and sucked her away.

He sat down in his easy chair, a red pencil and pad on the table beside him, and listened to the radio as the Red Sox lost again. His famous course, English 6, had named and attempted to digest the one hundred books God judged necessary. He planned to include, in his personal monograph (that was the final achievement and legacy of every Head before him), a copy of his list. He tried to recall the spirit of the complaints that had come from the students and female faculty. *Why no women?* Emily Dickinson was there, if they looked closely; Jane Austen less so. Wharton labored in dubious territory (New York), covered with greater strangeness by Henry James, though James did not, *enfin* (as James himself might have said), make the cut. Willa Cather's bohemian tales always charmed, but the Jewett girl covered territory he liked better. But if it came to that, he'd rather go back to Wharton's eccentric *Ethan Frome,* which he found less fine than three poems by Edwin Arlington Robinson. The female faculty had dominated every conversation from the moment they arrived: The curriculum must be made "relevant" and "diverse." What could be more elegant or diverse than Thackeray, or Shakespeare, or Conrad? His aunt Olympia, herself female, had taught him taste—*Tom Brown's Schooldays, Treasure Island,* Hawthorne, Shakespeare and the rest of the great English poets. Blake and Milton—the divines.

The holes in his mouth itched. (After decades of drinking coffee, his wife had suddenly refused the stuff—said it made her breasts itch. He couldn't stand that kind of talk.) His lost teeth lay in a silver candy dish. God shook them into his hand—his pearls. He sat in his chair with his teeth in his hands and watched flies buzz against the sealed windows. Why do anything now?

Because he was a tiger! (But he'd waited too long; they brought girls in.) He dropped the teeth back into the dish and took up his pencil and pad. He drew a column, Doric and stoic, and turned the capital into a man's head. He drew hair—and set the hair on fire.

The hills beyond the Wetstones' house were blue as city pigeons. What did he really want to say? The effects of his blood-pressure medicine, for example—a surging feeling. He only wanted to leave some impression of himself upon the world, to show things as they were.

He watched the flies buzz and butt against the window and counted the bodies crawling upward on the glass. Five, six—they were drawn to the light. Today's dying flies lay on their backs on the sill and rubbed their filament legs together. Yesterday's flies lay dead and dry, each pair of legs crossed over a black triangular belly. A new generation marched over the preceding one. (Gazing through the glass, beyond that valley of death, God saw his white birch trees gouged with canker sores.)

What would his wife put on a bloody mouth wound? A picture of Madeline's hands fluttered before his eyes, grains sifting down between her fingers: salt. He rose with trouble and poked around in the kitchen cabinets, whose blackened hinges wore the greasy deposits of years.

Salt. Would that be in a bottle? A jar? A dish with a spoon? Looking in the cabinet, he found garlic salt, celery salt. But he wanted a cardboard canister with a picture of a young girl on it. Here it was—salt. Salt rains; it pours. . . . He poured grains into his hand, clapped the hand to his mouth. Obliterating pain helped; it lifted the fog. Am I hardy and *hale*? he asked himself. The bone was strong, but the soft stuff that held the bones in place had worn down; the soft parts had worn away.

His teeth felt like chalk. He ground them down when he slept, as Dr. Dix had warned him not to. Dix had given God a rubber dam to bite, but he'd kept it in a drawer next to his bed the way a man might keep a pistol, imagining he wouldn't have to use it.

Red pencil still sharp in his hand (his habitual weapon, his rapier!), God plodded up the stairs, his hand on the rail, and reached the bonny nook finally. He sat on the edge of the bed and rested. Mrs. Graves's black binder sat on the blotter of the lady's tambour desk: his book. Groping in the bedside drawer, he found a floral bag of the kind his wife used to use for her specs. He opened the bag and let the object inside slip out.

He recognized the disembodied part immediately, assisted by fine print along the base. *The Vulcan. 100% nonporous silicone. Wash by hand using mild soap or in top rack of dishwasher.*

He turned the object around, observed its circumcised condition, its impressive size and substance, which combined the sensual texture and sheen of rubber with a sturdiness one associated with American-made products. A fetish, or a symbol of some kind—although what was a John Thomas, detached from a testicle, a symbol *of*? It was a deep, plummy red and had a slightly sticky texture that resisted pressure from his finger. He found its familiar oddness beautiful; the piece stirred him. (He wished he could tell Aunt Olympia.) He leaned back against the pillows on the bed, one cased and one bald, and rested. His chest heaved as if an ancient rock had been turned over and all the subterranean many-legged insects from the dark corners of his mind were scuttling for cover. But the rock turned; the lid lifted. God's eyes overfilled with water and he wept. Tears rolled down his cheeks, down his neck. He'd never felt more human.

His life, a dream thin as paper, hinted obliquely at what he might have been. Like a page torn from a glue binding, God began to peel away from the world. He would go into the darkness alone—and circumcised! (Though for this journey, he would not need the foreskin, the prostate gland; he would not require that appendage he referred to euphemistically as "myself.") His flesh was of no consequence; it would melt.

He'd made the original marks on 133 legal pads in what Mrs. Graves had criticized as a "gnomelike hand." She interpreted and translated in those places where he had been too close. God hoped that his marks would become real to the writer who made them march along the years, and to the printer who set and fixed them into permanence, and to the reader who read them. But he could not, himself, read the life in the work. At the bottom of the last page he wrote:

APPROVED—GB

He laid the red pencil and the silicone Vulcan in the drawer and made his way to the stairs.

He hit his head when he fell, said Dr. Wu. Part of him froze. He forgot how to eat and how to swallow.

Dr. Wu discussed the pros and cons of the feeding tube with EV and Mei-Mei Hellman, not because they had authority, but because they stood up in the waiting room when he entered. "Because we were like Everest," Mei-Mei said; "because we were there." Without the tube, God would die of pneumonia. With the tube, he could live until his heart failed.

EV and Mei-Mei agreed God wouldn't want to live such a circumscribed life. With the tube, a nurse would pump liquids into God, but he would never eat or drink again—no salted nuts, no crackers and cheese, no evening martini. When EV brought the decision—no tube—to Dr. Wu, he said, "Have you asked Mr. Byrd what *he* thinks?"

She leaned over the hospital bed where God lay with his eyes closed and said, "The doctor wants to put a feeding tube in you. If you agree, you'll never eat or drink again. But it will save your life for now. What do you say?"

God opened his eyes and wheezed. "I guess I'll live." Dr. Wu dropped the tube down, and sent him home with a nurse.

Delice Asgarali puts the kettle on for tea. "He's near the end, poor man," she says in her lilting island voice. "He tears at his bedclothes; he twitches in the night. He hasn't lost his will, though, and that's the great thing, EV." She puts on a mitt, opens the oven door and pulls out a sheet of cookies. She scrapes the cookies off the pan with a spatula, lays them one by one on a blue-flowered plate and sets the plate on the table.

Ms. Asgarali chooses a cookie, bites, frowns, chews. "He thought he walked home last night, all the way from town. How could he have done that? All along the highway? It's miles away! He asked for an egg, said he'd been walking all night. I said, 'Where do you think you walked to, Mr. Byrd?' And he said, 'I walked home from town. What else could I do?' And I said, 'What were you doing in town, Mr. Byrd?' and he said, 'I had a rendezvous.' I heard he hasn't been himself since he was circumcised. It's too much for a man this age. Any surgical procedure can be a shock, and this . . . well. The penis is so important to a man, don't you think, even toward the end of life?"

He'd walked eight miles in the damp, and caught it—Death—probably from the shock of the explosion during the revolutionary protests in town. The episode rattled him, especially bones and teeth.

Women threatened even from this distance to drown him out. He waited; all he had to do was lie and wait. It would come to him. He fetched up an image to keep him company: a blue day, the wind crisp off Squantum. The tide approached, withdrew. He waited on the shore in a watery memory.

He'd asked that the helping women wear their names on their breasts. He had too much on his mind to remember their differences. He sat for a few minutes at his India-rubber desk, or seemed to sit there, and sketched the shape he wanted for his gravestone in red pencil on the purchase order. (How wise he had been to buy early!) He wanted square corners. "No round," he wrote beside the square.

He glanced at the electric clock on the desk: 11:33 p.m. The hairs rose on the back of his neck: The red second hand spun toward twelve, then suddenly stopped, though the little machine continued to buzz in a live way. The red hand of time—stopped. Moments passed and God waited for a minute, two minutes. He held the pencil in his dead-looking hand. Then the red hand began again, dropping gracefully down, a controlled and elegant swoop from twelve to six. God bore down again on his pencil and wrote in the instructions field, "Slate stone, if possible; it lasts."

As God wrote, he slept, and as he slept he dreamed of a wall, a New England stone wall in which one hundred necessary books formed the stones. The wall had grown dangerously tall, the stones irregularly shaped, of different sizes, and so on, laid almost carelessly on top of one another without any mortar. Some had faces and names, but he could no longer read them. God crouched on one side of the wall, attached to it by a cord. The cord was structural, umbilical; his life fed the wall. He had seen one other wall like it, in photographs. People went there from around the world to touch the stones with their fingers, and leave their prayers in the chinks between the stones.

"Juice?" A regal, young, nut-colored nurse entered the room. A piece of torn masking tape on her bosom read DELICEASGARALI. Her face shone with estrogen. She flattened herself over God's body and poured the fluid into him.

The cord of human knowledge! One end of the cord stopped—here. DELICEASGARALI said, "Mr. Byrd, it's just your feeding tube. Does it feel like something sticking into you?" Yes, something was sticking into him—the cord of human knowledge that connected him to the stones.

Two undertakers in suits of midnight blue rolled God's body onto a stretcher and bore it away under a black blanket. They stowed his shell in the back of a van and drove up the hill toward the full moon. God watched from somewhere beyond; he saw everything. His point of view lived on, why not? Life rolled on, continuous; Michelangelo died at the moment Shakespeare was born. Death granted infinite freedom. No longer attached by a mortal cord, he could not act upon the world. His point of view grew less fervent; he cared less, and then he did not care at all.

He did not ride with the women in the car to St. Vitus. The polished chrome hubcaps neatly covered the nuts of the tires and met the rims in the shape of a cross. God rode here—in the wheels. The revolutions of the radial rubber tires, faithful Goodyears, were turns of the earth around the sun. He stood at the center of the revolutions that pulled him toward his final destination. He saw, from inside his chrome cross, the familiar maple and birch trees, glimpses of ocean, the first vistas of granite and sea foam after the marshy wetlands to the south. He saw the whole road; it was a century long and led to the nave at St. Vitus, where he must leave behind those who remained and roll on alone. He'd been granted this privilege—and did not question it—of riding to his own funeral in the eye of the wheel outdoors, while all the women, whoever they were, sat contained in the car above him, insulated and protected and out of it.

2005

Souls of the Drowned

The new Head, Dr. Ruth Brasile, ordered a hundred copies of Goddard Byrd's book, *The Venerable Head: A Self-Portrait of Goddard Byrd,* printed in time for graduation. The cover featured a woodcut—God's head—done by the New York artist Carole Faust, the first female admitted to Goode, who happened this year to be the graduation speaker. *The Venerable Head,* a handsome and distinguished product, turned out (at thirty-nine pages) more modest than the graduation program, a four-color job that contained advertising. The book had been a pet project of Mrs. Graves, God's longtime secretary; she was the one who distilled the bright points of his experience from the murky constellation of a century, turned 133 yellow legal pads of observations and impressions, lists of "essential books" by men, letters, articles in the *Head's Journal,* together with a rash of awkward arguments against coeducation that appeared in the *Globe* in the late 1960s and early 1970s. Mrs. Graves had turned it, turned him, into a coherent figure, or, as God would have said, "a figger."

Dr. Brasile presented copies of the book to the board of trustees, to the faculty and to Carole, the featured speaker. Carole spoke about her experience as the first African-American female to attend the school. She spoke of struggle as the only form of knowledge, and praised God for his commitment to conditions that made struggle morally obligatory. She cited W. E. B. DuBois, Langston Hughes, Zora Neale Hurston, Paul Robeson, Malcolm X, Toni Morrison, none of whom she had read in her time at Goode. The hardy assembly, over a hundred young men and women and their supporters, endured her brilliant talk through a sudden rainstorm that included apocalyptic thunder and even a few scratches of lightning across the leaden sky. The mortarboards began to take on water. Carole concluded:

> The question of influence is interesting. I was formed by anger. I raged against the then-Head with a force so passionate, it was indistinguishable from love. Even now, every decision I make comes from a sense of duty to the Head. If someone asks me out to dinner, I think, What would the Head say? (The Head would say, "There she goes, Carole Faust, whittling away her time in social life"—so I make it a point to eat, drink and be merry.) Anything the Head told me was impossible—a life as an artist, a life without children—I did that. When a voice in my mind tells me, You can't paint the way time speeds up and slows down, or You can't paint sorrow, or You can't paint Ecuador, it's the Head's voice I hear, his effete, attractive whine. This voice has lived in me since I was fifteen; it's as much a part of me as my own voice. The Head is in this way my inspiration. He is the source of my adrenaline, anxiety and rage—and the secret of my success.

Later, over coffee and cake in the castle, an old man wearing a plaid bow tie held forth to a knot of graduates, male and female, with an anecdote about the difficulties a new boy once had in God's class. "He was a public school boy," the man said, "but we all saw he had what it takes."

Someone said, "Who was Goddard Byrd?"

"Oh, the last of the single-sex heads."

"It's ironic, isn't it, the last holdout against women at Goode is memorialized by his former secretary, who, I heard, literally died at her desk writing the thing, and eulogized by the first female student at the invitation of a female head?"

"That tribute book? Can you believe it was hand-set in letterpress?"

The man turned and his hand appeared before Carole. She shook it. "Dick Whitehead," said the owner of the hand. He had soft brown eyes and a chiseled manner.

"I enjoyed your tribute," Dick Whitehead said. "Although if anybody asked me, taking God Byrd's oral English class made me what I am. It changed my life. We used to memorize twenty, thirty, forty lines a night—the Gettysburg Address, Lincoln's Second Inaugural, sections from the King James Bible, Shakespeare—just the widest range of thought. I want to tell you, I never liked it. I'm no effete intellectual. I was in industry. But in that class, I learned discipline. I learned to be prepared, to pay attention. Served me well in business."

"What business were you in?"

"Dog bones," he said irritably.

"What was the name of your business?" Carole asked. "Maybe I've heard of it."

Dick Whitehead acknowledged the insolence of the question.

"First company—Penzance Pet Products—was taken over by a conglomerate, which was good, so I started a company of my own. Whitehead Bones."

"Why was that good, having your company taken over by a conglomerate?"

His eyes narrowed. "More efficient distribution, lower overhead, better prices for you, the consumer."

"Is that good? When things are cheaper, don't people just buy more?"

"Are you some kind of Communist?" Dick Whitehead said.

Carole smiled. "Worse than that," she said.

After the reception, seventy-three of the one hundred copies of *The Venerable Head* remained under the folding chairs, where they lay sheltered and ruined in the grass. I know because I counted them as I gathered them up. Then I took them back to Mei-Mei's, where I laid them out to dry into swollen husks, which she kept for ten years. Carole Faust came back with us to spend the night. She'd offered to give me a ride back to New York in the morning.

It was God who brought and bound Carole and me together (her rage toward him against my fawning love), and we became friends, or rather, I followed her like a puppy, scratching at her with letters and e-mails and requests for advice, to which she usually responded.

I ran downstairs, then across the gray-painted porch and into the blowsy, leafy street. The air was hot and muggy, and so dense that the rain, though sluggish and irregular, seemed to be having trouble penetrating it. A small river of muddy water had begun to flow in the direction of the library. I jumped over it and stood on the corner, exposed, hoping she would see me.

The cars that passed revealed nothing but blurred faces behind windshields, sheets of water and wipers that swung back and forth across the glass. Thunder rumbled under my feet, rain ran down the back of my neck and a long bolt of lightning shot through the sky and landed somewhere beyond the library. My sense of drama swelled, and I thought, My life, my life, as if my cards had been dealt but not yet turned over.

I stood on the corner, becoming wetter and wetter, listening to the sound of rain hitting hollow-sounding things. Carole pronounced my name "Eve," and I could not bring myself to correct her, because by now it was much too late to correct her.

"Can I talk openly around your mother?"

"Of course."

Mei-Mei had a Rob Roy; Carole and I drank Shiraz. We three sat in Mei-Mei's three Windsor rockers, rocking.

"How have you *been,* Carole?" Mei-Mei asked in a concerned way, opening up small talk as she became expansive with her drink.

"Very well, though a little wrecked. I'm just getting over a sort of icky relationship."

Mei-Mei grimaced and knocked on the wooden arm of the rocker.

"My husband had cancer last winter, which was awful. He thought he was going to die, although he didn't—he just became impotent and depressed. So there was that, and finally I stupidly started this relationship—I have to say that because it was mostly *not* sex, thank God—with a woman who worked at my gallery. But you know, although I love women, and I do, I always have, there's something, I don't know, you find yourself just, I don't know, lying there with their fingers inside you, thinking, What am I doing here?"

Mei-Mei clucked sympathetically. "Oh, gee," she said. But this small confidence was enough for her; it opened up the possibility of going deeper. In the end, Mei-Mei told Carole the whole story—the German-made kayak, the delusional weather that March, the eight miles of rough water between Penzance Point and Capawak, the hero (described in the papers as "a hardy Danish nursemaid") who saw the boat capsize and swam a hundred yards in thirty-eight-degree water to save the other man—Carole's father, Rebozos. I know the story by heart—like all ghost stories, the story of my father's death must always be told exactly the same way. The fishermen of Capawak dragged the water for hours until they brought my father up—a boat hook caught him by his sneaker. He had a dollar in his pocket, a detail that caused my father's wealthy uncle Frank particular grief. The police identified Heck Hellman and called Mei-Mei. The call taught her that we could never rest, could never assume that anyone would come back. If you tell Mei-Mei, "I'm going outside to meet Carole Faust at her car," she'll say, "Be careful of the *street,*" and touch something wooden with her knuckles.

"May I have another drink?" asked Mei-Mei, interrupting herself.

"Me, too!" said Carole. "But keep talking."

I went out to the kitchen and found Mei-Mei's little urinal—a glass vase, actually—which held the generous dregs of her evening Rob Roy. I added ice and poured out a glass, then poured more wine for Carole and me. Carole didn't usually drink—she veered in and out of a form of spirituality that tolerated and forgave sexual indiscretion but took a hard line against alcohol. At first, this felt awkward, like a cultural difference between us, like Carole being black, or bisexual. But Carole rejected identity politics. She simply was herself—"just strongly male-identified. I like men *and* women."

When I came back with the drinks, Carole was leaning forward in her chair, her eyes fixed wide on Mei-Mei, who is a first-rate storyteller, especially of *this* story.

"It was raining—like today," Mei-Mei said. "Only winter, colder. I didn't beg him not to go—I didn't want to be that kind of wife, the kind of anxious woman his mother was. He told me they were just going to try out the kayak along the shoreline. And your father, Rebozos, I mean, *Archer*—well, it was, as you know, a very af*fluent* family. He was dressed for the weather. He had a life jacket. Heck didn't. No raincoat and no life jacket. The woman who saved him—I wish I could remember her name—said he was swimming. Heck didn't swim. Maybe he had hypothermia. He just held on to the overturned boat, touching it with his fingers. She saw Heck's fingers slip away from the boat. She saw him sink underwater."

But the usual story had veered off course. I saw Mei-Mei's hands, her fingers vertical, just touching the sides of an imaginary boat, not holding on at all. Her eyes were bright. "He didn't have a life jacket on?" I said.

"No," she said.

"You never mentioned that—the fingers on the side of the boat, the life jacket, the woman seeing him go under. You never told me that."

"Didn't I?" said Mei-Mei.

"Why didn't he have a life jacket?" Carole asked.

"Because we were poor," Mei-Mei said angrily. "Because we didn't have any money."

"I hear you," said Carole.

But I couldn't let go of this detail about the life jacket that was not a detail, that changed our whole story into a story about power and economics, about our lesser equipment and poorer tools. I'd misunderstood everything. "You never mentioned the life jacket," I said. "How come I never knew?"

"I never thought of it that way before," Mei-Mei said. "When Carole said that about the women's fingers—that gesture—I don't know, I was shocked. I thought of your father's fingers touching the side of the boat—not even letting go, just falling away. It freed me. It upped the ante."

Carole laughed, reached out and took Mei-Mei's hand in hers and held it, laughing.

The rain stopped; the sky lit up. I went to the kitchen to freshen our drinks. When I came back, Mei-Mei stood with Carole at the open window, pointing into the air.

"Look," she said. The sky had turned into lines of pink and bright orange, and thin clouds stood in an even queue, like dominoes. "Don't the clouds look like the souls of the drowned lined up waiting to be counted?" she said. "I think of all those people lost in that tsunami in December, all of them at once, so many.

See, there's the dog guarding the gate of heaven and the souls have to wait in lines on the horizon. They're even dressed in the sunny colors of those countries, waiting in the last sunlight over the water to be counted." She said, "Carole, dear, can you see how they're the souls of the drowned? Can you see their watery faces?"

Acknowledgments

Thanks to Randall Babtkis, Dorothy Cooke, Laurie Fox, Charlotte Gordon, Jordan Pavlin, Chessie Stevenson, Sarah Stone and Kate Walbert for their insightful reading, protracted encouragement and practical help. Parts of this book first appeared in *Five Fingers Revew* and *The Idaho Review,* to whose editors I'm grateful. For generous gifts of money, time and extraordinary spaces in which to work, I'd also like to thank the National Endowment for the Arts, the PEN/Robert Bingham Fellowship Award, the California Arts Council, the Ucross Foundation and the Djerassi Resident Artists Program.

A NOTE ABOUT THE AUTHOR

Carolyn Cooke's short-story collection, *The Bostons,* was a winner of the 2002–2004 PEN/ Robert Bingham Fellowship Award, a runner-up for the PEN/Hemingway Foundation Award and a *New York Times* Notable Book. Her fiction has appeared in *AGNI, The Paris Review* and *Ploughshares,* and in two volumes each of *Best American Short Stories* and *Prize Stories: The O. Henry Awards.* A recipient of fellowships from the National Endowment for the Arts and the California Arts Council, she teaches in the MFA writing program at the California Institute of Integral Studies in San Francisco.

A NOTE ON THE TYPE

The text of this book was set in Monotype Sabon, a typeface designed by Jan Tschichold (1902–1974), the well-known German typographer. Based loosely on the original designs by Claude Garamond (c. 1480–1561), Sabon is unique in that it was explicitly designed for hotmetal composition on both the Monotype and Linotype machines as well as for filmsetting. Designed in 1966 in Frankfurt, Sabon was named for the famous Lyons punch cutter Jacques Sabon, who is thought to have brought some of Garamond's matrices to Frankfurt.

Typeset by Creative Graphics, Inc., Allentown, Pennsylvania
Printed and bound by Berryville Graphics, Berryville, Virginia
Designed by Maria Carella